THE SECRET OF THE LIGHTHOUSE

By

Rick Farren

www.journeypublications.com

Journey
Publications

First Edition: August, 2004

ISBN: 0-9748087-3-3

Printed in the U. S. A.

Dedication

To those who have always been intrigued by lighthouses,
known as *America's castles*.

Special appreciation to my wife, Ann, my most loyal supporter,
my best critic and closest friend.

Special thanks to Judy Giere and Bette Ruggles whose
gifted editing helped make this book a reality.

Dickey Denton sat patiently in his sixth grade classroom, watching the clock on the wall as the minute hand loudly ticked off the remaining few minutes of the end of the school year. It had been an interesting year for Dickey, starting with a perfect losing record for his school soccer team. He usually played forward and believed he was pretty good, until playing the position of goalie, he missed a shot at the net from a ball kicked exceptionally hard, and on target, by a member of the other team—and of all people—a girl. Thankfully, the other team had no better record than his school, so no one ever mentioned the loss…or the manner of how it occurred.

Thanksgiving festivities had been held at Dickey's house, and as usual everyone showed up. His aunts and uncles were all there, along with his cousins, but best of all—his Grandpa. He always loved it when Grandpa came to his house—it was always special—*very special*. Grandpa would plop himself down in the big soft easy chair by the fireplace, unbutton his holiday vest and light his hand carved pipe. Dickey loved the aroma of the sweet smelling tobacco as the blue swirls of smoke curled lazily towards the ceiling and then wafted up the chimney flue. He vividly remembered his conversation with Grandpa that day as clearly as if it had happened only yesterday.

"Where's Kelly?" Grandpa had asked winking at him with his ice blue eyes.

"In her room on the computer I think," Dickey replied. "At least until Mom calls her to come help set the table."

"Hmm," Grandpa mused watching the flames dance around the crackling logs and licking their way around the iron grate. "We never had computers when I was your age," he said shaking his head and smiling, "Actually, all we had was a telephone and a radio. We'd listen to the radio shows, especially on Sunday nights, like 'The Green Hornet' and 'The Shadow.' Grandpa sat back puffing on his pipe and then looked reflectively at Dickey. "Would you like to hear a story, before dinner, about something that happened not that far from here? It's a story I heard when I was about your age."

"Sure," Dickey quickly agreed sitting on the edge of the brick hearth near his grandfather's feet. There was something magical about Grandpa's stories, and he felt fortunate to have a grandfather who knew how to tell a good story. "What's the story about, Grandpa?"

"Do you think your sister would like to hear the story too?" Grandpa asked.

"I dunno," Dickey replied shrugging. "Want me to go ask her?"

Grandpa nodded and re-lit his pipe. It wasn't uncommon for Grandpa to relight his pipe three or four times, and make that 'puff, puff' sound with his lips as he always did.

In a flash Dickey returned sitting on the edge of the hearth.

"Kelly said she's online with a girlfriend. She said she'd rather do that than listen to a story."

"Okay," Grandpa mumbled, shaking his head thoughtfully as he stroked his beard. "Too bad, because she might enjoy the story. It's about a girl around Kelly's age."

Oh my goodness, Dickey thought. *A story about a girl?* He shuddered at the thought. After all, it was a girl that made the winning goal in his soccer game, and made him appear as though he couldn't successfully defend the goal for his team. He swallowed hard trying not to show his displeasure.

"What is it?" Grandpa asked, noticing the look of concern on Dickey's face.

"Nothing," Dickey replied, reluctant to tell his grandfather that girls weren't one of his favorite subjects.

His grandfather settled back in the chair. "When I was a young boy about your age," he began, "we lived on an island just off the coast of Cape Cod. It wasn't a large island; it was actually pretty small, but a nice place for a young boy to grow up. I used to enjoy going over the large hill near our house and down the wooded path to the beach to watch the fishing boats dragging their nets. I had to travel to school each day to the mainland on my Dad's boat, even in the worst of weather. Your great grandfather, my father, was a good sailor and a fisherman by trade. It's hard work being a fisherman, and he would be out every day before sun up, tending to his nets and getting his boat ready for the day. He was a good man, very strong, with great big calloused hands and a quick smile. He had a thick mop of red curly hair that glistened in the evening sunlight when he was coming back into port. Other fishermen often said they could always see my father coming, his red hair shining like the sun. My father always found humor in everything, and he was a great storyteller. One of the best, but that was partly due to his heritage. He was part Irish you know."

"I know," Dickey remarked. "Mom and Dad told us that our great grandfather came from a coastal town around here somewhere." His brow furrowed for a moment. "I can't remember..."

"Mayport," Grandpa said. "You should know that—it's just down the road from here. It was a big fishing town in those days, that's for sure, and I assume it still is." He re-lit his pipe again and puffed a couple of times while staring at the fire.

"Grandpa?" Dickey asked, when his Grandpa paused. "What about the girl? You started to tell me a story about a girl who was close to my sister's age."

"Oh sure, sorry. I got to thinking about something else." He leaned forward and patted Dickey on the knee and smiled. "I lost my train of thought." He tapped the ashes from the bowl of his pipe on the edge of the hearth examining the pipe like something was still left inside.

"Grandpa?" Dickey asked again.

"Yes, Dickey—I know. I'm getting to the story. I didn't forget. It just takes me a while to collect my thoughts and accurately recall the story as I had heard it."

He settled back in the easy chair and stuffed fresh tobacco into the bowl of his pipe. It was a beautiful white pipe, hand carved, in the shape of a Native American warrior's head. Grandpa struck a long wooden match on his boot and lit the pipe. Dickey waited anxiously for him to begin.

"It was sometime around the turn of the 20th century," Grandpa began. "Actually, in the year 1904, when a young girl made a life altering decision. My grandfather told the story to his son, my father, when he was just a young boy."

Dickey's chest pounded with excitement waiting patiently to hear the story, gazing into his Grandpa's blue eyes. Dickey had a story to tell as well. It was about a gold button he had found—the one off of Peg Leg Pete's frock coat—but it could wait. Dickey wasn't much for story telling, but after the time he spent with Grandpa on Angel Island last year it was probably time he broke down and told him the story of that night, and how they came to be rescued. Dickey had the inscribed gold button safely hidden away in his special secret hiding place. But he decided he wouldn't go into the story—not at this time—not now. First he wanted to hear the story about the girl.

"Are you listening?" Grandpa asked, tapping Dickey jokingly on his head with the stem of his pipe.

"Yes, Grandpa. I'm listening."

"Are you?" He questioned, his eyes narrowing as if he didn't believe him. "You appeared to be daydreaming."

"No, Grandpa, I'm not. I'm listening. You said your father told you a story that his father had told him about a young girl around the turn of the century."

His grandfather frowned as he stared at the crackling fire. "Yes, yes, that's right," he replied smiling. "Thank goodness you've got a good memory. I just wanted to see if you were paying attention." He chuckled and set his pipe down on the end table. "It seems that a twelve year old girl by the name of Eliza Tuffett, the daughter of a lighthouse keeper, signed on as a deck hand on a trade ship without her mother or father's knowledge, *or* permission."

"Holy cow!" Dickey exclaimed. "She left home without her parents permission?"

"She most certainly did," Grandpa replied.

"But didn't someone notice she was a…girl, and too young to be a seaman?" Dickey asked.

"No. Not at all. You have to remember in those days no one cared about underage help, so long as a person could work long hard hours. To keep them from finding out, she wore her hair tucked up under her cap easily passing herself off as a young boy. She could work just as hard as any man, rig the masts, splice rope better than most, and haul supplies until the sun went down. She was a pretty girl and tall for her age. My father told me her most distinguishing feature was a beauty mark, almost like a small mole," he said touching his index finger to his face. "Right about here on her left cheek. She lived with her parents in a lighthouse where, like I said, her father was the lighthouse keeper. It was a different and lonesome way of life for Eliza since she was an only child, and never had many friends. After six years of formal schooling, she abruptly quit school, and one night slipped out of the lighthouse after dark leaving her parents a note. It was a cold and blustery December evening, just before Christmas, that Eliza took her father's skiff from their dock and rowed half the night across the bay to the docks on the other shore. Once there, cold and hungry, she signed on as a deck hand on a trade ship proving her worth in no time as an able bodied seaman. As I heard the story, the trade ship left port on Christmas Eve bound for South America, the South Pacific and the Orient. It seems Eliza was always intrigued with visiting other continents and learning about the people. Her parents were brokenhearted upon reading the note she had left stating she was off to see the world. From that day on, they kept a light burning in the lighthouse window that faced the ocean as a vigil for her safe return. No one knows for sure, but I guess the meaning of the light was to guide her ship home safely."

"And did she return home safely?" Dickey asked breathlessly, his eyes wide with wonder. "What happened to Eliza, Grandpa? Do you know all this because she kept a diary or something? Where was the lighthouse? Was it near here?"

"Gee," Grandpa exclaimed grinning. "You do have a lot of questions tucked away in your head, don't you? Yes, the lighthouse is near here, and I'll bet you can guess which one it is." His blue eyes twinkled waiting for him to answer.

Dickey stared back almost afraid to reply. And then, with what little voice escaped his lips, he asked, "Is it Rocky Neck Lighthouse?"

Grandpa nodded. "Eliza began keeping her diary, or as she called them, her journals, when she was about ten years old. I know all this because her journals are stored in my attic."

"Dickey!" His teacher, Miss Simpson spoke sharply startling him. "Are you listening?"

"Yes ma'am. I am," he replied, shaken by her voice. He realized he hadn't been listening at all. He had been remembering the story Grandpa had told him last Thanksgiving.

The day was warmer than normal for mid June and Dickey could smell the flowers that had bloomed just outside the classroom window.

The school caretaker was cutting the grass for the first time, his mower making that low humming sound as it always did. It was as if the mower signaled the beginning of an adventure for the next two months.

Bobby Page, the boy in the seat next to him was a funny kid and always kept Dickey, as well as the rest of the class, laughing. Miss Simpson referred to Bobby as the *class clown*, whatever that meant, but Dickey was certain it wasn't a good thing. It was just the way his teacher would say it to Bobby that made Dickey realize he didn't want to be known as the class clown.

Today, Bobby had taken advantage of the warm aromatic breeze drifting though the open window and was sound asleep on his desk, his head resting on his chubby forearm. He was snoring ever so slightly, not loud enough for Miss Simpson to hear, but loud enough to cause Dickey to glance at him. Dickey looked away peeking again at the clock on the wall. *Less than five minutes to go*, he thought, the anxiety of being out of school making his chest rise in anticipation. Summer was coming and he was anxious to put away his schoolbooks and enjoy the warm carefree days, the beach, camping, and fishing.

His teacher was wishing the children an enjoyable summer, but to be careful riding their bikes and to always wear a helmet. She also said something about how they should spend part of their summer vacation reading some of the classics, like The Three Musketeers, Charles Dickens, and Huckleberry Finn.

Dickey didn't hear much of what she was saying since he had been daydreaming about having the next two months off and all the fun he'd have. His older sister, Kelly, now in middle school, had been released from school two days earlier. She had poked fun at him for having to go to school for two extra days. It wasn't fair, he thought. Not fair at all. *What could Kelly do with two extra days off from school? She didn't even know how to fish*, he thought shaking his head. Even if she did, she wouldn't catch anything—least of all a big bass like he had caught with Grandpa two years ago. Kelly was scared to death of worms, and couldn't even bait her own hook. And then he smiled remembering the time he hid some worms in her underwear drawer. Boy! Did she ever cry that day. *There's nothing to baiting your own hook,* he reflected thoughtfully remembering what his Grandpa had told him. "Just bend the worm in half and stick the hook through both sides. It won't hurt him a bit because worms don't feel a thing."

How silly of Kelly to feel the way she does, he thought, and to be afraid of baiting her own hook. There was nothing to it.

"Girls," he mumbled under his breath. "They're afraid of everything including spiders, getting dirty, and worms."

How quickly he had forgotten his own fears that magical and stormy night last year while stranded on Angel Island.

"C'mon sleepy head!" Dickey's mother announced walking into his room the next morning. "Time to get your bones out of bed." She snapped opened the blinds allowing the sunlight to pierce the darkness. "Just because it's school vacation doesn't mean you can spend the next two months sleeping your life away.

Dickey blinked, squeezing his eyes shut, and groaning loudly, as he pulled the covers over his head.

"No groaning and moaning, Dickey," his mother said laughing, as she stepped over a pile of discarded clothing. "Just get up and come down for breakfast. And while you're at it, you can think about cleaning up this pigpen you call a room. I would prefer it if you would do it today before you go out."

"Where's Dad?" Dickey asked, his voice muffled under the blankets.

"Already at work," his mother replied. "Just like always. It's almost ten o'clock and most people are up and have their chores done long before now." She tapped him on the foot as she left, closing the door behind her.

Dickey rubbed his eyes and stretched, wondering what the first day of school vacation might bring, other than cleaning his room. He didn't see the need to hang up his clothes when he was just going to put them on again the next day. After all, they weren't dirty, just rumpled. It seemed that his mother never had to ask his sister to hang up her clothes. But what his mother didn't know was that Kelly hid her clothes on the floor of her closet—not out in plain sight.

Dickey loved his room. It was his own secret haven—his refuge—clean or not, and it provided him a special hideaway. He had acquired his room quite by accident, two years earlier, when his sister took the larger of the two rooms claiming, *and* whining, that she needed more closet space than he did. He imagined it was probably because she could hide more clothes in it out of their mother's sight. He willingly agreed to the room change since it was the corner room of the house with double windows on both sides. He liked more light—the more light the better—except when his mother yanked opened the blinds just about blinding him. He rolled over and tucked his arms under his head looking at the shelf that ran between the windows to his right all the way to the far wall. It held most of his important memorabilia—not all—but most of his good stuff. It held the autographed baseball that Grandpa had given him when he was five years old with the scribbled fading signature of the New York Yankees great baseball player, Joe DiMaggio. The baseball held the place of honor and Grandpa had painstakingly carved a beautiful mahogany wooden base for it. He told Dickey the story of how he had obtained DiMaggio's signature after he caught a foul ball the slugger had hit into the stands at Fenway Park in Boston. Grandpa had said it was sometime in the late 1940's, which to him seemed like ancient history. "The 1940's was a time," Grandpa had said, "when kids could walk home alone from school, buy penny candy at the corner store, and would listen to the exciting radio shows at night before bed."

He closed his eyes and his mind drifted back to the lighthouse. The one Grandpa had mentioned last Thanksgiving, that was two miles away out at Rocky Neck. The lighthouse had intrigued every school kid since the beginning of time. In class, they had studied about lighthouses, as they were an integral part of Cape Cod. Miss Simpson had explained that in the late 1800's and early 1900's, without the aid of electricity, their beacon lights served as navigational guides and were illuminated by whale oil, wood, or paraffin. The keeper's duties, among many others, were to trim the candle wicks, so that the reflection off the lens would stay as bright as possible and could be seen by the ships at sea. She told the class that fog was the foremost enemy of ships; since fog was unpredictable and could obscure anything that might damage or sink a ship. She said that to reduce the potential for shipwrecks along the coast, the first audible foghorn was installed in Boston Harbor in 1719. Dickey didn't find a lot of things exciting about school, but he was fascinated with lighthouses, and his teacher's description. She explained the primary purpose of a lighthouse was to save lives. She also told the class that lighthouses were known as *"America's castles,"* and as fascinating as they were, living and tending a lighthouse was a lonely and isolated way of life.

Rocky Neck Lighthouse was a forlorn, aging structure sitting virtually unattended on a short spit of barren land overlooking Muffin Bay. Although abandoned by its keeper, the beacon was now automated, being maintained once a month by the Coast Guard. From what he had heard from others, the bay acquired its name from the founder of the town.

Legend had it that Muffin Bay referred loosely to its similarity to the shape of freshly baked muffin tops, and the shape of the land surrounding it. The lighthouse was also a legend around the town of Crystal Falls. It was a place that most people in town never ventured to go—even the tourists—even on a bet. Its only visitors were the boys in town who used it as a back drop for hide and seek, fighting off imaginary pirates trying to plunder the town, and scaring the local girls on Halloween. And yet, to his knowledge, no one had ever mustered up the courage to go inside. Rocky Neck Lighthouse, at almost 100 feet tall, stood 60 feet higher than the tallest building in the town. Due to cutbacks in funding and staffing, the last lighthouse keeper left in the early 1980's causing the lighthouse to fall into a state of disrepair, until the Coast Guard took over. Over the past few years the Coast Guard had made minor improvements to the structure.

Dickey's hometown of Crystal Falls was a small, intimate town of about 2,000 residents, most of whom made their living in the fishing and lobstering business. There were some however, like his father, who held white-collar jobs but worked out of town. Most of the residents all knew one another and pretty much kept to themselves, except for the community Saturday night bean suppers at the church, or attending a local sporting event. The town sat on the south coast of Cape Cod Massachusetts, ten miles north of the nearest large town of Mayport. Josiah Wheeler, a prosperous whaling ship captain had founded the town in the early part of the 19th century. He also built a rambling, pretentious, 14-room mansion on the highest hill in town where he and his wife raised their seven children. Josiah was in his late fifties when he lost his life aboard his whaling ship 50 miles west of Nantucket Island during a freak blizzard in 1890 and his body was never found. Rumors still abounded that his wife,

Elizabeth's spirit, still walks the "widow's walk" of their house at night, especially during a full moon, watching for Josiah's return from the sea. Dickey had never seen her "spirit," but many of his friends claimed they had. He wasn't one to believe everything he heard, and yet, he wasn't about to criticize or doubt his friends until he actually witnessed her *spirit* for himself.

During the summer his time was consumed with sand lot baseball games, riding his bike to the beach, visiting his friend Charlie, and checking on his treasured gold button that his secret hiding spot had guarded for over a year. During the winter, school took up most of his time especially with his bewilderment in trying to understand math and word problems. But most of all he loved the holidays when Grandpa came to visit.

"Dickey!" His mother yelled from downstairs shaking him from his reverie. "I hope you've got your room cleaned up, because breakfast is on the table!"

He threw back the covers swinging his legs over the side of the bed and sat for a moment staring absently at his toes. "Ooh," he groaned loudly. "It would be so nice just to stay in bed."

Ten minutes later he walked into the kitchen and plunked himself down at the table. A healthy serving of pancakes and sausages were already steaming on his plate and the aroma was magnificent.

"Where's Kelly?" He asked, eagerly digging into his breakfast.

His mother was standing at the counter waiting for the toast to pop up. "She'll be down soon," she replied. "She's cleaning her room."

Her remark hit him in the gut. Kelly always obeyed their mother, and did as she was asked. He imagined it was mainly to make him look bad. *And was she was good at it*. He always obeyed his mother as well, but sometimes it just took him a little longer.

At that moment Kelly walked in. "Good morning Mother," Kelly said taking her seat at the table across from Dickey, and placing her napkin on her lap. Dickey looked askance at her as he cut up his sausage. "Good Morning, Dickey," Kelly said coolly as she poured a substantial amount of maple syrup on her pancakes. She then asked Dickey something he couldn't quite make out.

"What'd you say?" He asked with his mouth full.

"I said," she replied evenly. "Have you cleaned your room like Mother asked?"

"I'm going to," he replied, almost spitting out his sausage. "I just need some time."

Kelly chuckled under her breath setting the syrup bottle down while watching the amber colored sticky mass flow slowly into the crevices of her pancakes.

"Clean your room before you go out," his mother said to him, placing a platter of toast on the table. "Now eat up both of you, and no more teasing back and forth." She placed her hands on her hips and stared at Kelly. "And you, young lady, it's none of your concern whether your brother has cleaned his room or not. That's my business, and you'd be well advised to mind your *own* business."

Dickey could hardly control himself. It wasn't often that his sister got reprimanded, but when she did it was worth every minute of it. He stifled a laugh almost choking on his sausage.

An hour later, after picking up his room as best he could, he was on his bike pedaling as fast as possible to Charlie's house, a ten-minute ride away. The chain on his aging bike squealed loudly as he pedaled faster and faster.

He loved visiting Charlie's house because his mother always had fresh baked chocolate chip cookies, and spending time with him was always an adventure. Charlie's house sat high on a sea grass covered knoll behind a massive sand dune overlooking Muffin Bay. From Charlie's bedroom window he could see Rocky Neck Lighthouse. On a clear night when the stars dotted the sky like diamonds on black velvet, Charlie told Dickey he could see a distant brilliant light in the lighthouse. He said the bright light was in a small window that faced the ocean across Muffin Bay—not the rotating lighthouse beacon—but a smaller, much brighter one.

Charlie Sullivan was Dickey's best friend, and was always there when he needed him. He was a true bookworm, and a consummate reader of science fiction. He was tall and skinny, taller than Dickey by a few inches, with a shock of red hair and glasses. If there was a way to do something, even when it might stump another classmate, Charlie could usually figure it out. The summer before he and Charlie had built an elaborate two-story tree house in Charlie's backyard. It was nestled high in the bough of one of the tallest oak trees. It took them almost two months to build it, working diligently afternoons and weekends. Dickey had the carpentry skills, while Charlie designed the layout and wired his radio on the second floor. He was someone that Dickey could always count on and they spent countless nights in the tree house, tucked in their sleeping bags, and making up stories, even though Dickey wasn't good at challenging his own imagination. Last year his father had threatened to improve Dickey's vocabulary and imagination by making him learn one new word each day, and at the end of the week to use the words he had learned in a story.

Thank goodness, Dickey thought. His father must have forgotten because the subject never came up again.

The first floor of the tree house functioned as both a cooking area and their sleeping room. They had a small portable stove on which they'd make fried bologna sandwiches, and boil water for cocoa. The stove was just like the one his Grandpa had the night they were stranded on Angel Island. A shiver rolled through his body just remembering that night, and he tried to put it out of his mind. At night, four candles provided the only light in the tree house, and the shadows thrown off by them caused his and Charlie's images to dance eerily against the plywood walls. Charlie had once offered to wire electricity off an old car battery so they could install an electric lamp, but Dickey nixed the idea, saying the tree house would lose its original purpose of being a secret hideout. They consumed their delicious fried bologna sandwiches for lunch, and the rest of the afternoon devoted their attention to making small but necessary adjustments to their hideaway.

Later that afternoon, with most of the work completed, Dickey said, "It's got to be after four o'clock by now."

"So what," Charlie responded without looking up as he sat cross-legged with a pencil and paper designing something that resembled a kitchen cabinet.

"So, it means I have to get going home for supper in a little while."

Charlie didn't answer but simply glanced past Dickey as if he was thinking about something important. He put his pencil down and locked eyes with his friend. "You have to come back here tonight after supper."

Dickey's eyes narrowed as he returned Charlie's vacant stare. "Why?"

Charlie simply grinned and said, "Just come back after supper. It's going to be a real clear night and there's something I want to show you."

"What is it?" His heart was beating like a drum. Charlie had definitely captured his attention. *Was it something magical?*

"Just come back after supper."

Dickey thought about what Charlie had said as he pedaled home arriving just in time for dinner. He ate in relative silence, trying to imagine just what Charlie had in mind.

It was just past seven-thirty when Dickey, totally out of breath, pulled up behind Charlie's house on his bike. He propped up the bike near a large oak tree and looked around anxiously. Not seeing Charlie in the yard, he climbed the makeshift ladder to the tree house and peered into the first floor. Still not seeing Charlie, he climbed to the second floor. Still— no Charlie.

Where could he be?

Dickey couldn't believe his parents had allowed him to go back to Charlie's house after dark, but he understood they trusted him to do the right thing, and to return home at a reasonable hour. He had promised he would.

"Dickey!" Charlie's voice broke through the darkness breaking Dickey's concentration. "I didn't think you were coming back." Charlie was standing on the first floor staring up at him. "Light the candles," he said, "so we can see what the heck we're doing. Do you have any matches?"

"Yeah, they're here on the shelf I built." Dickey replied, striking a long wooden match and touching it to the wicks of the four candles. They had been careful not to put the candles near any of the wood, and had them carefully secured in small glass bowls lined with tinfoil.

"Mentioning the shelf you built," Charlie remarked grinning. "You'll be impressed to see what I built." He climbed to the second floor of the tree house and faced Dickey. "You're not the *only* carpenter in this deal. I know you think I can only wire things together, and make old radios work, but check this out!" Charlie reached up and grabbed a piece of sash cord dangling just above his head and yanked on it. When he did, an overhead trap door dropped down revealing a narrow set of stairs leading upwards into the night sky.

"What…is it?" Dickey asked dumbfounded, staring up into the darkness.

"It's a trap door, and a way to get to the highest part of the tree," Charlie replied beaming. "Isn't this the coolest thing you ever saw?"

"Yeah," Dickey whispered, awestruck at Charlie's ability to build such a contraption, especially without his help. Charlie was good at many things, but most of them revolved around either mechanical or electrical problems, nothing that remotely resembled anything to do with carpentry. Dickey grabbed a small flashlight from their makeshift emergency survival kit and pointed it up through the trap door into the darkness. "Wow!" He gushed excitedly. "Unbelievable! You built this? How come I didn't see it earlier?"

"Yup! I finished it after you left. You didn't notice because I had just finished it, and the cord wasn't in place. But, stand by my friend," Charlie remarked chuckling. "You haven't seen anything yet. C'mon, follow me." He mounted the small rickety ladder as Dickey followed closely behind until they reached the top of the tree house. They had built it solid—real solid—solid enough to easily support both of them. Dickey had dragged the half-inch plywood sheets all the way from Charlie's father's workshop, but it was worth the struggle. The strength of the structure allowed both of them to stand on the roof without it sagging an inch.

It was pitch black as they breached the night, reaching the roof of their hideaway, and Dickey stood silently beside his best friend.

"What now?" Dickey whispered, shining the beam of the flashlight around but not seeing anything out of the ordinary. And then he noticed it. It wasn't anything that would catch one's eye right off the bat. It was just a normal everyday wooden six-foot stepladder propped on the roof of the tree house. It was leaning awkwardly against the gnarled trunk of the large oak tree.

"Gimme your light," Charlie said, taking Dickey's flashlight and shining it past the step ladder up the tree trunk until the beam stopped at a crude plywood slab nailed between two large branches. The plank was just above the top step of the stepladder. "C'mon," Charlie said excitedly, "Let's go up so I can show you something."

"Umm…I don't know," Dickey replied, hesitating as he stared up into the black abyss. "It doesn't look…"

"It doesn't look…what?" Charlie asked warily, squinting at him as he pushed his glasses up to the bridge of his nose.

"Stable—I guess," Dickey admitted sheepishly. "It just doesn't look stable."

Charlie simply laughed and climbed the ladder, the flashlight beam dancing in the night sky until he reached the plywood plank. "See!" he said looking down at Dickey and patting his hand on the wood plank while squeezing himself into a cross-legged position. "Steady as a rock. Climb up!"

"Why?" Dickey pleaded, feeling as if he were being pressured into something he really didn't want to do. "Tell me why I should be doing this?"

"Because you'll never believe what I'm going to show you. Come on, Dickey, don't be a wimp. Climb up here!"

Reluctantly, he climbed the ladder, and after a few hesitant crab like moves, he slid onto the plank beside Charlie.

"See," Charlie said handing the flashlight back to him. "Piece of cake, right?

"Yeah, if you say so," he replied indifferently. He couldn't believe he had actually climbed up the ladder to the rickety piece of nailed wood. He thought, *whatever Charlie wanted to show him, it better be good and worth the trip up.* "So, what's so important to show me that I had to climb way up here?" He held on so tightly to the edge of the makeshift seat, his knuckles were turning white.

"Didn't I do a good job building this?" Charlie asked patting the board affectionately. Without waiting for Dickey to answer, he continued. "I call it the crow's nest, just like they had on the old sailing ships where the lookout would climb up and look for land, pirate ships or whales."

"Well, I don't think we're going to see any of them tonight," Dickey replied skeptically. "It's dark for crying out loud! What can we possibly see? I don't see a thing, and I'm going to climb down the ladder now before I fall off and crack open my skull."

"Not so fast," Charlie said grabbing his arm. "And turn off your flashlight. There's plenty of light, it's almost a full moon."

"Why turn off my flashlight?"

"You'll see. Just turn it off."

Dickey complied, and in the darkness all that could be heard were the night peepers chirping their song, along with a few old bullfrogs croaking the night away in the nearby marsh.

"Okay," Dickey said. "It's off. Now what?"

"Are your eyes adjusted to the dark yet?" Charlie asked in a loud stage whisper.

"I guess so—why?"

"Look over there low in the sky, right over Muffin Bay." He said pointing straight ahead. "Do you see that real bright star?"

Dickey strained his eyes, peering into the night, and as much as he hated to admit it, he couldn't see the star. "No…I don't think so."

"Follow my finger," Charlie said holding his arm in front of Dickey's face. "See it now—the real bright one?"

"Oh yeah—I see it now."

"Good. Now look straight down from that star, on this side of the bay. See that huge old mansion, the one with all the windows?"

"Not really."

"Look again!" He declared pointing. He was beginning to sound annoyed. "The house that's sitting way up high on that hill to the left of Rocky Neck Lighthouse."

"Oh yeah—okay, I see it now. It's the big house that has something that looks like an iron pointed fence around the top of it."

"Right!" Charlie exclaimed. "Now look closer. You'll never believe what you'll see."

Dickey rubbed his eyes yawning loudly, uninterested that he was really listening to Charlie ramble on about nothing. He thought at this point he'd rather be home, rather than sitting on a plank halfway up a tree at night staring out across Muffin Bay.

"Look closer," Charlie urged.

He did, and that's when he noticed something—something that appeared rather unusual. It looked like a person walking around the top of the house. *It can't be a person*, he thought, and then shook his head figuring his mind was playing tricks on him. He squinted even harder and looked again. The moon illuminated a figure on the roof that appeared to be wearing a long dress or some sort of a gown.

"Is that a person I see walking around on the top of the house?" Dickey asked. His mouth went dry reminding him of the time he inhaled sawdust by mistake in his father's workshop. Charlie simply smiled, feeling as though he had revealed a secret of which only he had knowledge. "Is that a person?" Dickey asked again. And then it dawned on him and his eyes widened. It was the house he'd always heard the stories about, the one where the ghost of the ship captain's wife, Elizabeth Wheeler, walked the "widow's walk" at night watching for her husband's return from the sea. It was also the only house in Crystal Falls where the children were not allowed to go on Halloween. A shiver ran through him and goose bumps popped out on his arms.

"That's right," Charlie said. "It's the Josiah Wheeler house, and the story is that his dead wife walks the widow's walk when the moon is full watching for her husband's return."

"Holy cow!" Dickey whispered mesmerized at the sight of the apparition. "I just never thought there was any…"

"Any what?" Charlie asked. "Any truth to the stories we've heard all our lives about the ghost that walks the roof of the Wheeler house?" Dickey nodded unable to speak. "Well," Charlie said, quite pleased with himself. "Now you've seen her for yourself." He paused a moment, and then continued. "And, if you look over there," he said pointing to the right just past the Wheeler House, "you'll see Rocky Neck Lighthouse—way out on that spit of land. They say it's taller than—"

"Any building in town," Dickey remarked interrupting him. "I know. I've heard that. It's also the one we can see from your bedroom window, right?"

"Yeah…but—"

"My Grandpa told me the story about it last Thanksgiving," Dickey said interrupting him again. "But I'll bet there's something you *don't* know about the mystery of the lighthouse?"

"*Mystery?*" Charlie asked, the words catching in his throat.

Ah, Dickey thought. *I can finally tell him something he doesn't know.* "Look over there at the lighthouse," Dickey said. "Do you see the rotating beacon on the top?"

Charlie nodded. "Yeah, sure I do. So what? That beacon has been rotating since the beginning of time, at least as far as I know."

"Watch, Charlie," Dickey cautioned, "and wait until the beacon flashes on the other side out towards the ocean, and then look at the small window on the second level beneath the beacon. It's the window on the side that faces Muffin Bay and the ocean."

A moment passed and the beacon turned dark toward the land, and Charlie stared as hard as he could at the window. "There's a light in that window," Charlie whispered breathlessly not taking his eyes off of it. "It's a real bright light—but very small. It looks like the same light I can see from my bedroom. Remember? We've seen it before. But I don't understand where it comes from. I mean there's no one living there anymore." He looked at Dickey waiting for an answer.

"I'll make a deal with you, and if you agree," Dickey said. "I'll tell you a story about a young girl who lived there many years ago, and left home to sail the seven seas. *And* I'll tell you why that light is there."

Without hesitation Charlie quickly agreed. "What's the deal?"

"The deal is," Dickey said, wrapping his leg around the first rung of the ladder getting ready to climb down, "that we climb down now to the tree house, and get the heck off this plank!" They both laughed as they climbed down and closed the trap door behind them.

Even though Charlie had shared his experience of the mystery of the Josiah Wheeler mansion, Dickey had spun his own web of intrigue regarding Rocky Neck Lighthouse.

He knew now he had Charlie in the palm of his hand.

The next morning Dickey woke up early, long before his mother was due to come in to shake him out of bed. Lying there he thought about what he and Charlie had seen the night before from their tree house, and what tonight might bring. They hadn't developed their plan as yet, about venturing off to Rocky Neck Lighthouse, or to the Josiah Wheeler house, but he knew it would be something he would love to do. It would certainly be something none of his classmates had ever done, and there was a mystery to explore. He was still amazed that Charlie had the skills to build the trap door to the roof of the tree house, since Charlie's abilities certainly didn't lean in that direction. He was much better at wiring up a DVD player then he was working with a screwdriver.

Dickey looked at the clock on his bedside table. It read seven-thirty.

He figured if he could get his chores done at a reasonable time, he'd be able to go to Charlie's house and work on perfecting the tree house even more than it was. And then by sundown he'd be able to tell Charlie the story of Eliza Tuffett, much as his Grandpa had told it to him.

The chores around Dickey's house seemed endless, the grass had to be cut, and his room, a mess as usual, had to be straightened up.

Ten minutes later, having dressed in a rush to be able to finish his chores, he entered the kitchen finding a note on the table from his mother.

Dickey:
Dad and I went to the store to finish shopping for our camping trip. Kelly is still sleeping so don't wake her. She was up late finishing packing for our trip. Hopefully, you'll be up before we get back. Get your clothes and sleeping bag ready to go, and never mind your chores for now because we're leaving as soon as we get home. You can do your chores when we return. We hope you're looking forward to camping in the White Mountains, as it should be fun. Dad's all excited about teaching you how to hike the rugged mountain trails in New Hampshire.
Be back by ten o'clock.
Love, Mom

"Oh my Goodness," Dickey muttered under his breath, slumping noisily into a kitchen chair. He stared at the note disbelieving what he was seeing. "Camping?" He whispered, swallowing hard and staring at the note again for what seemed like forever. He was totally stunned. "I'd completely forgotten we were going camping."

Dickey had just finished straightening up his room, and collecting his camping gear stored in the attic, when he heard the front door slam.

"Dickey!" His father hollered up the stairs. "We're home! I hope you're ready. Is Kelly up yet?"

Before he could answer, Kelly yelled from her room. "I'm up and showered and ready to go!"

Sure, Dickey thought. And I'm sure her room is neat as a pin as usual. That big closet is a wonderful thing to have. And then he had an idea. Not a great idea—but an idea.

And, if there was any way he could get out of going camping, and join Charlie to investigate Rocky Neck Lighthouse and the Josiah Wheeler mansion, he had to give it a try. Kelly had a phone in her room, and if he waited until she went downstairs he could sneak in and call Charlie. Maybe Charlie had a way to help him get out of going camping, but he'd never know unless he tried. He opened his door a crack and peeked out seeing Kelly leave her room. Running on his tiptoes in his stocking feet, he dashed into her room; his heart beating like a drum, and quietly shut the door behind him.

"Dickey!" His father hollered again. "Come on down! It's time to go!"

He dialed the phone faster than he ever thought he could and waited while it rang, once, twice, three times. "Come on," he mumbled urging someone to pick up the phone. And then the recorder kicked in. Discouraged, and at a loss as to how to get out of the trip, he hung up.

"What's the matter with you?" His father asked, stuffing the last of the cold packs into the cooler, as Dickey entered the kitchen. "I thought you'd be excited about the camping trip. Why the long face? After all, it's only our second year with the camper and you seemed to enjoy our trip last year."

"Yeah, I did," Dickey replied trying to put a smile on his face. "It's just that Charlie and I had big plans for tonight, and I hate to leave him wondering."

"Oh, I'm sure he'll understand," his father replied indifferently as he collected plastic cups and plates off the table placing them in a large carton. "Whatever you and Charlie were going to do tonight, I'm sure can wait until you get back. If it'll make you feel any better, call him and tell him you'll be away for a few days."

Dickey shook his head, thinking, I can't believe Charlie is going to have to wait five days before I can tell him the story of Eliza Tuffett.

"Right?" His father asked hefting the oversized picnic basket off the kitchen counter.

Dickey looked up at him as he finished the last of his cereal. "What Dad?" He asked. His mind drifted to the bright light in the window of the lighthouse, and the mystery surrounding why it was there. He also couldn't get the vision out of his mind of the woman who walked the widow's walk of the Wheeler mansion.

"I said," his father repeated, "I'm sure whatever it is you and Charlie were going to do tonight can wait until we get back."

He felt his heart sink at the thought of being gone for five days, but he was out of options. "Yeah—sure Dad—no problem."

Five days sharing a camper with Kelly wasn't his idea of a wonderful time, but his choices were limited. Actually his choices were slim to none.

"Finish your breakfast," his mother said glancing at the kitchen clock. "Time's ticking away and Dad wants to be on the road before eleven. Kelly already has all her stuff in the camper. And," his mother said as an after thought, "if there are any doors upstairs that are closed please open them so the air can circulate."

Dickey pushed back the chair and without a word went upstairs and collected his camping gear. He gave one last cursory glance at the phone on Kelly's bedside stand as he passed her room, and then thought better of trying Charlie again. Five minutes later he was helping his father load and organize the pop up camper. They were ready to go. He knew from their trip last year it would take them at least four hours to get to the campsite in New Hampshire.

The first hour in the car always seemed to pass by rather quickly, but it was the final three hours that were the worst, trapped in the rear seat of their SUV beside Kelly. He and his sister constantly fought for space control, neither giving an inch, both complaining vociferously to their parents.

It rained three out of the five days at the campground. Dickey and Kelly, in order to appease their parents, agreed to a truce in their arguing and actually got along fairly well the last few days. Meeting other kids their age at the campground recreation hall helped put enough space between them to curb their petty quarrelling.

Late in the afternoon, five days later, they pulled in the driveway of their home.

His father shut off the ignition and let out a long sigh. "We're home!" He announced sounding tired. "It's nice to get away, but it's also nice to be home." He clapped his hands together and said. "Okay kids. Time to get things cleaned up and put away."

And time to call Charlie, Dickey thought. He must think I dropped off the face of the earth.

"You know where the dirty clothes go, right kids?" His mother said as they walked into the kitchen. Her question was rhetorical since he and Kelly were well aware of where the hamper was, and what had to go into it. His mother always asked the same question when they arrived home from anywhere, and Dickey believed it was more a reminder of what they had to do. "And," his mother continued, "stick around and don't go anywhere before supper. It'll be ready in less than an hour, and it's going to be an easy supper because I'm tired. I'm not cooking a big meal tonight."

"Can I go out after supper and see Charlie?" Dickey asked hopefully.

"We'll see," she replied busying herself in the kitchen.

"But it doesn't get dark until about seven thirty, and—"

"Dickey!" His mother said, locking eyes with him, her hands planted firmly on her hips. "I said, *we'll see*."

He knew when she looked at him the way she did—she meant it. He wasn't about to challenge her decision if he knew what was good for him. Without another word he lugged his camping gear upstairs and threw his dirty laundry in the hamper.

At precisely five thirty, Dickey, Kelly and their parents sat down to eat. They chatted about their trip and what could've been better, or different, and what they might do the next time instead. They all agreed of everything on the trip, the weather left a lot to be desired. But overall they had a good time and couldn't control the weather.

Dickey was unsure how to approach his parents on the issue of going to see Charlie, as he sat picking away at the green bean salad.

"You're quiet tonight, Dickey," his father observed. "Do you feel okay?"

Dickey nodded. "I feel fine, Dad."

"No he doesn't!" Kelly piped up glaring at Dickey from across the dinner table. "He wants to go out tonight and see his friend Charlie, and the camper isn't even cleaned up. Nothing has even been put away yet."

His father chuckled as he wiped the corners of his mouth with his napkin. "If that's what you're thinking, son, forget about it."

Dickey felt like leaping across the table and knocking his sister to the floor. *Why was she always interfering in his business?* It was none of her business what he had intended to do after supper. Now she had planted a seed of doubt in their father's mind. He cringed thinking what might come next. He felt he had to at least ask the question.

"I was hoping to go to Charlie's tonight, Dad. If I can, I promise I'll take care of everything tomorrow."

His father laughed again, shaking his head, while pushing his plate aside. "There's an old saying that goes, never put off until tomorrow what you can do today." He glanced at the kitchen clock. "And mentioning that, we've got a good two hours of daylight left, which is plenty of time to get everything done. You can go see Charlie tomorrow and tell him all about all the hiking we did, and the pictures you took in the mountains. But not tonight, because we all have to chip in and get this work done."

Dickey felt his stomach sink. Another night would slip by before he and Charlie would be able to sneak up to the lighthouse, and possibly the mansion. He didn't think he could stand to wait even one more day.

"May I be excused?" Kelly asked, refolding her napkin and setting it beside her plate.

"Not so fast, young lady," her father said. "You're not exempt from the cleaning detail. Get the bucket out from under the sink and you can help your brother scrub the floor of the camper."

Total silence filled the room as Kelly sank back into her chair, her mouth hanging open.

It was all Dickey could do to keep from laughing right out loud. If he had to stay home and work on the camper, it was worth it to have his sister working beside him, just as hard. Her face reddened as she glanced at Dickey, and he simply smiled back at her. His expression said it all. She tried to beat him out of going to see Charlie and now she was stuck working as well.

By the time they had finished, shortly before eight o'clock, he figured it wasn't even worth calling Charlie. He'd call him in the morning and explain about the missing five days.

After brushing his teeth and getting ready for bed, he made one important inspection of his most prized possession. First he made sure his bedroom door was shut and then walked over, and kneeling down, he reached under his dresser. The cardboard box was still there, taped securely where he had placed it, and where it couldn't be seen. He had never told anyone about the box and the special secret it held. It was his special secret that someday he'd share with his grandfather as he had promised.

It held the gold button he'd found that morning on Angel Island over a year ago—the button off the flowing green frock coat of the pirate—Peg Leg Pete.

"Well, you were right, Mom," Dickey said after cleaning up his dishes from breakfast the next morning.

"I was right about what?" She asked, loading the dishwasher in her own meticulous manner.

"My chores. You were right about them. You said they could wait until we got home from camping." He stood on his tiptoes and looked out the kitchen window into the backyard. "Jeepers!" He exclaimed. "The grass must be five inches high."

"I'm sure it is," his mother replied casting a quick smile in his direction. "Did you expect the grass cutting fairy to come and cut it while we were away?"

"I guess I better get started if I'm ever going to finish my chores today," Dickey remarked. "Do I have to do anything to the lawnmower first, Mom, before I try and start it?"

"I don't think so," she replied matter of factly, as she wiped down the counter tops. "Your father said he checked it and it has enough gas and oil." She paused and looked at him. "Do you want any help getting it started?"

He shook his head. "No thanks. Dad has shown me the right way, and it shouldn't be a problem. It seems fairly easy."

"Okay, if you feel comfortable doing it yourself. Otherwise, I'd be glad to come out and lend some muscle," she remarked with a grin. "Oh, and also, Kelly is going to help you rake up the cuttings as soon as she's through breakfast."

It's about time she did some work around here, he thought. I never saw anyone rake as slowly as she does.

"What's the matter?" His mother asked. "You look as if you have a question on your mind?"

"No, Mom, no question. I was just thinking about something."

"Well, you better stop thinking and get going, because time's a wasting, young man. The grass isn't going to get cut all by itself." She paused looking down at Dickey's feet. "And don't cut the grass in your sneakers young man. Remember what Dad told you. Put on your heavy boots and safety glasses so your feet and eyes are protected."

"I will." He started to go upstairs to change and then paused on the first step. "Can I go over to Charlie's house tonight after supper?"

"I guess so. I don't see why not, so long as you get your chores done in time."

Fifteen minutes later, dressed in his clunky boots and safety goggles, he went out and opened the shed. He was hoping none of his friends came around, since dressed in his boots and goggles he looked as if he had just stepped off an alien spaceship. He hauled the heavy self-propelled lawnmower out of the shed, and with some difficulty rolled it to the edge of the lawn. He placed his foot on the housing and yanked hard on the cord. Nothing. He yanked even harder the second time until he thought his shoulder would come out of its socket. Again nothing. He wiped his brow and glanced quickly at the kitchen window hoping his mother wasn't watching. He knew he could do it himself. It was hot and he imagined it had to be in the low 90's. His father's words came flooding back to him. *Don't keep yanking the cord if it doesn't start after two pulls.* He had cautioned Dickey regarding the proper way to start the mower, and one thing he didn't want, was his mother coming out to help. *"If you keep yanking the cord you'll flood the engine,"* his father had warned. *"If you do, it'll never start."*

Frustrated, Dickey sat down on the grass to wait it out, and give the engine a rest before trying again. He figured it couldn't hurt. After all, a rest never hurt anyone or anything.

"What are you doing sitting down?" Kelly hollered as she came out the back door and walked across the lawn. "Mom sent me out to help you rake, but you haven't even cut the grass yet. So tell me what I'm doing out here roasting in the hot sun like a walnut, when nothing's been done?"

"I'm giving the engine a rest!" He shouted.

"Ha!" She exclaimed sarcastically, chuckling under her breath. "It looks to me like you're giving *yourself* a rest, not the lawnmower."

Kelly had an extraordinary knack of being able to aggravate him, no matter what the situation might be. She walked over and squatted down beside the lawnmower looking at the motor housing for a long serious moment, and then tinkered with a couple of moving parts. She shook her head in mock disbelief, while she giggled and placed her hand over her mouth.

"What is it?" Dickey asked irritably, while glaring at her. "What are you laughing about?" He was hot as the dickens, and the last thing he needed right now was his sister poking fun at him.

"It would probably be a good idea to open the choke to that mark that says, *full,* before you try and start it," she remarked, this time laughing right out loud. She stood and walked over to the garage leaning against the doorframe. "Call me when you're ready and the cutting is all done. Until then, Dickey, I'll just hang out here and relax in the shade, because it looks like it's going to be a while before you're finished."

Her assessment of the problem, sad as it was, he thought, was indeed true. And because of it he felt stupid and couldn't even face her, *or* get off the ground to stand up. He watched Kelly roll her eyes, eventually walking back to the house and slamming the screen door behind her.

"Oh my goodness," he mumbled aloud. "I can't believe she noticed that I didn't have the choke in the right position." He waited until she was out of earshot and then reached over and moved the choke to the full position. He grimaced, realizing Kelly was right. One yank on the cord and the engine leapt to life. As angry as he was at his sister for showing him up because of his mechanical ineptitude, at least he'd be able to finish his chores in time to see Charlie.

Thirty minutes later he was finished and hollered for Kelly to come help him rake. While he waited, he chugged a few large mouthfuls of ice water from the container his mother had set out for him on the back porch. Eventually Kelly came out slamming the door behind her, demonstrating that she was clearly annoyed at having to help him, especially in the heat.

Forty-five minutes passed as they raked without speaking to one another, and then Dickey eventually broke the ice. "I'm sorry I was grouchy," he admitted. "You were right about the position of the lawnmower choke."

She shrugged and mumbled a quiet acceptance of his apology.

That afternoon he was busy. He had a scout meeting in order to prepare for the national scouting Jamboree in two weeks, and he had a three o'clock Karate lesson. It was just after four o'clock when his mother picked him up, and by the time they arrived home and he showered, it was almost dinnertime.

Just after five o'clock, he heard his father's car pull in the driveway. He figured he'd wait until after they ate before asking his father if he could go to Charlie's house. He knew his mother and father liked their quiet time together when he arrived home from work to discuss what went on during the day, and to relax over a fresh brewed cup of coffee. He knew better than to ask too many questions until his father had taken off his tie and jacket and had time to relax.

Shortly before six o'clock, his mother called Dickey and Kelly to dinner.

"And what did you two do today?" His Dad asked as they ate. He always seemed interested in what he and Kelly had done, or what plans they may have had. After their family discussion they finished dinner in relative silence.

After dinner, Dickey and Kelly helped clean up the dishes, and he finally mustered up the courage to ask if he could go to Charlie's house. His father glanced quickly at Dickey's mother for reassurance, and she nodded her agreement.

"Sure," his father said. "I guess so. Is it that important you see him tonight?" Before he could answer, his father continued. "I assume you got your chores done?"

His mother jumped in on the conversation telling his father that he had cut the lawn, and that he and Kelly had both raked. His mother agreed that Dickey needed some time to be with his friend.

"Okay," his father agreed. "You can go to Charlie's house. Just be home at a reasonable hour. Let's say nine o'clock."

"I will Dad," he replied anxiously. "I promise!" He dashed into the den and picked up the phone dialing Charlie's number. Charlie's father picked up the phone on the second ring and Dickey asked if he could speak to Charlie. A moment went by before he came on the line. "Charlie? It's me—Dickey."

"Where the heck have you been?" Charlie asked sounding aggravated. "I thought you were coming over last week? I haven't heard from you all week. I called you two or three times. Were you away or something?"

"Hold on a minute, Charlie, will you? For crying out loud! Take a breath and listen to me. I forgot we were to go camping, and I tried to get hold of you, but your recorder picked up instead." He went on to explain his absence talking about the camping trip, his chores, and his afternoon activities. Then he asked the important question. "Charlie," he whispered looking over his shoulder to make sure his parents weren't within earshot. "What if I come over tonight and we check out the Wheeler Mansion? I'm eager to check out that woman walking on the roof."

"She's not *walking on the roof*," Charlie said correcting him. "She's been known to walk the widow's walk during a full moon like I told you, watching for her husband to come home from the sea."

"Okay—whatever, but can I come over?"

"Sure, I guess so. But you made me a promise when you were here the last time when we were in the tree house."

"I did?" He asked trying to recall their conversation.

"Yep," Charlie declared. "If we check out *anything* tonight, it'll be Rocky Neck Lighthouse, and that bright light in the window."

"Oh…yeah…I remember now, but I'd really like to—"

"No way, Dickey!" Charlie remarked adamantly. "You promised you'd tell me the story of the girl that left her home at the lighthouse to sail the seven seas. And while we're at it, we might as well go and see for ourselves what's up with that bright light in the window."

Reluctantly he agreed, telling Charlie he'd be over in fifteen minutes. He hung up and braced himself against his mother's recliner trying to catch his breath. It was true that he had promised Charlie he'd tell him the story, as he had heard it from his grandfather. But there was no way he had enough courage in his soul to actually go into the lighthouse. He felt trapped. He was the one who had initiated the story of the young girl who left home to sail the seven seas, and now Charlie wanted to investigate the light. He knew there was no way out now. He had to go. Never in his wildest imagination did he ever think Charlie had the nerve to do such a thing, or for that matter, even remember the promise. But then again, he never thought Charlie could build a trap door in a tree house either. He sighed heavily, his heart pounding at the thought of what they were about to do, as he climbed the stairs to his room to get ready to go see Charlie.

It would be a night he would never forget.

Dickey peddled his bike up the Sullivan's long and winding driveway. He dismounted, propping it up as he normally did, against one of the large oak trees in the back yard. If Charlie was anywhere, Dickey imagined, he'd be in their tree house. *Where else would he be?* He's probably fussing with something electrical, like an old radio that is well beyond repair.

He dashed across the expansive manicured lawn reaching the tree house in record time. His heart was beating like a drum trying to think of how he could talk Charlie out of going to Rocky Neck Lighthouse. Nothing came to him. Listening to the story, related by his Grandpa, was one thing—walking into the mouth of the lion's den, and skulking around checking out the lighthouse was something else. Frustrated that nothing had come to mind as a way to get out of going, he climbed the make shift ladder to the first floor of the tree house and stuck his head into the semi-darkness. Wide-eyed he looked around.

"Charlie?" He called out in a harsh whisper. "Are you in here?" His voice echoed inside the plywood structure.

"Yeah!" Charlie called out from above. "I'm up here on the second floor. Come on up."

Dickey climbed the four narrow steps to the upper level and peeked through the hatch. "What are you doing?" He asked noticing the four candles burning brightly. Charlie was hunched over the small shelf in the corner that doubled as a workbench and a lunch table.

"I'm working on an old toaster my parent's were going to throw out," he replied without looking up. "I'm almost finished."

"What's the matter with it?" He asked, pulling himself up to the second level.

"It will toast just fine," Charlie replied, "but it wouldn't pop up the toast. So, as a result the toast just sits inside and fries until it looks like a hockey puck." He put down the screwdriver and pointed to the crude little window in the tree house overlooking his parent's house. "See that extension cord over there hanging inside the cut out window?"

Dickey looked and sure enough there was an orange cord dangling inside. "Yeah, I see it. What about it?"

"Pull it all the way in and hand it to me." Dickey did as he was asked. "Okay," Charlie said exhaling heavily. Beaming, and obviously proud of what he expected he had accomplished, he stood, rubbing his hands together. He grabbed the end of the extension cord with one hand, and with the other, held the cord to the toaster. He turned grinning at Dickey. "Do you know what they call this?"

Dickey's brow furrowed, unsure of what he meant. "An extension cord?"

Charlie burst out laughing. "No," he said catching his breath. "I *know* it's an extension cord. What I mean is, do you know what they call what I'm about to do?"

Dickey appeared perplexed and didn't answer. Charlie always had a way of posing a question that at best was confusing.

"Plug the toaster in to see if it works without electrocuting yourself?"

Charlie smiled and said, "Precisely, my friend. Precisely." He plugged the toaster cord into the extension cord and inserted a piece of white bread. "Ah," he said pushing down the cooking lever as delicately as if he were launching a lunar rocket at the NASA Space Center. "They call this *the moment of truth.*"

The two of them stood riveted, watching the toaster in anticipation, as it appeared to be toasting while at the same time making a strange clicking noise. A minute went by, and then the metallic snap of the toaster popping up the piece of crispy brown toast caused them to celebrate.

"I knew it would work!" Charlie remarked exuberantly extending his arms over his head, his fists clenched, as if he'd just thrown a no-hitter ballgame. "I knew it would work!"

"You are amazing," Dickey remarked giddily, patting him on the shoulder. "I don't think there's anything in the world you can't fix."

"I know," he remarked folding his arms jubilantly across his chest. "I am good!" They both laughed at his bravado and then Charlie turned serious looking at Dickey. "What do you think, Dickey?" He asked with a troubled squint. "It's getting late and before you know it, it'll be time for you to be getting home. That is," he continued stumbling over his words, "what I mean is, before we complete what we intended to do tonight, *and* what you agreed to tell me."

Oh no, Dickey thought. Charlie hadn't forgotten the promise as he had hoped he would. His blood ran cold thinking about what he had promised regarding the story of the girl who went to sea. *How could he get out of it?*

"Sure," Dickey mumbled. "I did promise to tell you the story, and—"

"*And?*" Charlie asked. "Don't forget we agreed to go to Rocky Neck Lighthouse tonight to check out the bright light in the window."

"Well, I…think I really only agreed to tell you the story of the girl as my grandfather told it to me. I really didn't agree to—"

"Come on," Charlie said interrupting him. "Let's go up to the roof of our tree house first and check out the lighthouse before we go." Before Dickey could object, Charlie had already scrambled up the pull down ladder of the trap door and was out of sight. Reluctantly he followed, noticing Charlie sitting high above him on the narrow board in the bough of the tree. "The light is still there!" Charlie exclaimed excitedly pointing in the direction of the lighthouse on the edge of Muffin Bay. "Just like usual."

"Great," Dickey replied under his breath unenthusiastically. "That's just wonderful."

"What'd you say?" Charlie hollered down.

"Nothing," he mumbled. "I said, that's great, but I think I have to be getting home."

"Not so fast," Charlie said bouncing down the ladder to the roof of the tree house. "You just got here and we're going to the lighthouse tonight—like it or not, my friend. You can tell me the story your grandfather told you while we're on our way. I'll blow out the candles and we'll get our bikes." He hurried by Dickey scrambling down the hatchway to the bottom floor.

In minutes they were on their way, navigating the narrow dirt pathways that led from Charlie's house, past the sand dunes toward Muffin Bay. Dickey was wishing he were anywhere but here, peddling slower and dropping behind in hopes that the lateness of the hour would change Charlie's mind. Charlie just kept pedaling.

"Come on!" Charlie yelled over his shoulder. "You're not keeping up! We'll never get there before dark at this rate."

I can only pray that's true, Dickey thought dejectedly as he picked up the pace.

Ten minutes later, with the lighthouse in full view, Charlie pulled his bike over and rested it against a large boulder near an intersecting path. Dickey pulled in behind him hoping his delaying tactics had worked.

"What is it?" Dickey asked. "Why'd you stop?" It was important he give the impression he still wanted to visit the lighthouse, so Charlie wouldn't suspect his real reason for slowing down.

"Because I want to hear the story about the girl before we get there," Charlie replied. "It makes it all the more exciting."

"Why? What's the difference if I tell you the story now or later?" Dickey asked, and then a thought struck him. "How about we go back to your house and I tell you the story there? We can do it right in the tree house. That way I'll be closer to home when I have to leave." It sounded like a workable plan.

"No way," Charlie replied assertively, shaking his head. "We're already here, and we're not going back now. Plus, I'm not going into the lighthouse until I know what you know. That's why!"

"It's not so much what I know," Dickey remarked, "but what I've heard from my grandfather. You have to understand that what I know is not first hand information." He took a deep breath and sat down heavily on the edge of the boulder. "My Grandpa heard the story about the girl from his father."

Charlie's eyes narrowed as he looked at him curiously. 'What's the matter with you?"

Dickey shook his head. "I guess I just believe my grandfather, and maybe I'm just a little, what do my parents call it? *Apprehensive* about going into the lighthouse."

"That's the whole point, Dickey. Don't you see? We've always used the lighthouse as a base of fear, a place to hide, and someplace to scare the girls on Halloween, but we've never gone inside. It's our chance to see if that girl's spirit actually haunts the lighthouse." Dickey sat speechless—somewhat stunned at the thought that this bizarre adventure might actually come to pass. Charlie sat down next to him and playfully nudged him on the elbow. "Now tell me the story about Eliza Tuffett."

"Okay," he replied indifferently, his eyes remaining fixed on the ground. "But you've got to remember it's what I heard from my grandfather. Like I said, it's not something I know about from first hand knowledge."

"Sure—sure, whatever," Charlie replied dryly. "Just tell me what you know, or what you heard from your grandfather, will you?"

Dickey tipped his head back looking at the dusky early evening sky. He was stuck—there was no way out now. He drew in a deep breath and began. "The girl's name, as you already know, was Eliza Tuffett, and she was about a year older than us at the time she left home. Her father was the keeper of Rocky Neck Lighthouse, and she was an only child, and lived there with her parents. Grandpa said she was tall for her age—and pretty—but," he shrugged grinning, "my Grandpa, thinks all girls are pretty. I have no idea why. Unless a girl can build a workbench or change a tire—"

"Dickey!" Charlie interrupted, his tone sounding exasperated. "Never mind about that! Just tell me the story."

"Yeah, the story," Dickey sighed. "Grandpa told me she had beautiful auburn hair, and a beauty mark right here on her cheek." He tapped his index finger on his left cheek just as his grandfather had.

"What the heck is a beauty mark?" Charlie asked appearing bewildered.

"I didn't know what it was either," Dickey admitted, "until I asked my Grandpa. He said it's kind of like a mole."

"Yuk!" Charlie exclaimed scrunching up his face. "That sounds wicked ugly. I'll bet the boys in town weren't chasing her around after school. No wonder she lived in the lighthouse where no one could see her."

"Don't be so cruel, Charlie," Dickey remarked, a look of disapproval crossing his face.

"Sorry," Charlie remarked frowning. "I didn't mean it that way. I was just kidding. An uncomfortable moment went by and then he said, "Go on with your story. I'm listening."

Dickey glanced at him and continued. "Anyway," he began again. "Grandpa said Eliza Tuffett attended grade school right here in town, and for the most part stuck pretty much to herself. It seems she was intrigued with ships—particularly sailing ships—and the mysteries of the other continents, and the people."

"How does your grandfather know all this stuff about her? Did he read a library book about her life?"

Dickey shook his head. "I don't think there is a book about her. I think most of what Grandpa knows is from what he's heard over the years, and the journals she kept."

"Journals?" Charlie asked wide-eyed. "You mean like a diary or something?"

"Yeah, I guess so." Dickey replied looking around furtively as if he were afraid someone might over hear his next statement.

"What is it?" Charlie asked whispering. "You look like you've got something else on your mind? Is it about her journals?"

Dickey nodded. "There is something else. But you can never tell anyone. Do you promise?"

"I promise. Cross my heart!" Charlie remarked hurriedly as if the moment would drift away like the morning fog. His eyes were wide with anticipation as he ran his index finger in the sign of an X across his chest. "I really do promise!"

"C'mon—Jeepers!" Charlie said urging Dickey to tell him the story he'd heard from his grandfather. "Are you going to tell me about Eliza Tuffett's journals or not? I mean sometime before it gets dark," he remarked sarcastically, "and before we get to the lighthouse?"

Dickey could tell by the tone of Charlie's voice that he was becoming irritated at his delaying tactics, and just wanted him to get on with the story. Dickey was still sitting on the boulder hoping that time, and the setting sun, would both slip away quickly enough so he could go home.

"I'll tell you on the way," Dickey replied glumly, as he stood and picked up his bike.

"No!" Charlie barked, stepping in front of Dickey's bike and gripping the handlebars. "You have to tell me *before* we get to the lighthouse! After all, you promised! It's not the same telling me the story while we ride our bikes."

He was beginning to whine, and it was the one thing Dickey disliked about him. It was a bad habit of his, and one that carried over even when they played sports. If Charlie missed scoring a goal in soccer, he'd whine that someone got in his way, or tripped him. In baseball, if he swung at a high and outside fastball that no one could have possibly hit, he'd whine that the ball was inside the strike box. Either way, he was still a good friend, his best friend, but he wished Charlie's parents would cure him of his incessant whining.

Dickey couldn't believe this was happening, but he couldn't blame Charlie for feeling the way he did. After all, most of it was his own fault since he was the one who started the whole thing by telling Charlie there was something he'd be interested in hearing about the girl in the lighthouse. Now he was going to pay for it. Going to the lighthouse was the last thing he wanted to do, but he couldn't see a way out. It was out of fear that he never ventured to the lighthouse, and the image in his mind of the spirit of Eliza Tuffett residing there. The mere thought of her haunting the lighthouse sent chills up his spine.

The sun, what was left of it, was slowly sinking in the western sky, *too slowly*, and the wind had definitely changed. The air had grown cooler, and had shifted, not the warm southwesterly breeze it had been earlier. It was now blowing in across the marshes that formed a crescent around the western tip of Muffin Bay. A chill rippled through his body. In the last few minutes the sky had turned a picturesque shade of violet, streaked with crimson, the time of day Dickey treasured most.

"Well?" Charlie asked smugly, aware he had won the challenge. "Tell me what happened, like you promised, about the girl from the lighthouse."

After a long moment, Dickey relented, laid his bike down on the sand and sat down on the large boulder.

"Okay, Charlie. I'll tell you, but remember you promised that if I do, it's between you and me. You crossed your heart and swore to keep the secret."

"Yeah, yeah, I remember," he replied with a guarded smile. "This is just too cool to pass up." Excitedly, he rubbed his hands together. "Now tell me."

Dickey was stuck and he knew it. It wasn't bad enough that his best friend was coercing him into going into the decrepit, supposedly haunted, lighthouse, but now he had to tell him the story of Eliza Tuffett and her private journals. It was clearly evident there was no way he was going to slide out from underneath this one. Like it or not, he made a promise and he had to keep it. That's what they taught him in scouts—keep your word—be truthful and honest. He thought for a quick moment trying to figure out a last ditch effort to resolve his predicament.

"But," Dickey said hopefully, calling upon his last resort. "If I take the time to tell you the story now, we'll never get to see the inside of the lighthouse. What I mean is, it'll be too late at that point, and I have to be home at a reasonable hour or my father will kill me."

Charlie rolled his eyes, pushing his glasses up to the bridge of his nose. "You know that's not true, and that's not a nice thing to say. You're being much too dramatic about this whole thing. First of all, your father's not going to kill you, and you know it. Secondly, you'll be home in plenty of time. If you just stop stalling and tell me what you know, we'll still have time to investigate the lighthouse before it gets dark." He stared hard at Dickey and then asked, "How long can it take for you to tell me about her journals, or diary, or whatever you called them?" He raised his eyebrows in anticipation waiting for Dickey's answer.

"Okay," Dickey replied realizing his options had run out. He felt defeated. If he told Charlie the story now or later, it really didn't matter. Dejectedly he stared at the toes of his sneakers thinking how to begin; just as a tiny sand crab scooted by, pausing momentarily, and then scurried off into the sea grass. "Grandpa told me it all happened sometime early in the twentieth century," he began slowly. "Around 1904 I think he said, but I can't recall exactly."

"It doesn't have to be exact," Charlie interrupted through clenched teeth. His patience was beginning to wear thin. "Just tell me the story about Eliza!"

Dickey glared at him, asking him not to whine and then continued. But not before he checked to see how low the sun was on the horizon. If he could just hold out a little longer, he thought, things might be different, and he'd have to be heading home.

"Like I said," Dickey began again. "It was sometime around 1904 when Eliza Tuffett disappeared from her home at the lighthouse." Charlie was intrigued, caught in the intensity of the moment. He sat down on the boulder beside Dickey, his eyes wide with wonder waiting for him to continue. "Grandpa told me that he has her entire collection of journals. There's got to be dozens of them, maybe even more. He told me they're all stored in his attic."

"*Dozens* of her private journals?" Charlie asked blinking with surprise.

Dickey nodded. "Yes. He said they go back to when she was ten years old, and all the way through her adult life."

Charlie was captivated, his mouth hanging open. "What do the journals say?"

"I can't remember all that Grandpa told me," he remarked, his brow crinkling in thought. "Let me see. He said her journals told of how she was an only child and grew up in Mayport on a small chicken farm that she and her mother cared for by themselves."

"Where was her father?"

"Away most of the time. He was a commercial fisherman and then later, sometime before she was born, he got his sea captain's license and captained trade ships to South America and to the Orient."

"Golly!" Charlie gushed. "Then what?"

"It seems from what she wrote, her father had some kind of an accident on board his ship and had to give up his life at sea. Grandpa said her journals explain that Eliza's father took a year off after his accident and worked at odd jobs in boat yards repairing fishing nets and the like. The year she turned ten, the keeper of Rocky Neck Lighthouse, a crusty old guy with an artificial hook on one hand, mysteriously disappeared. No one knew how or why—he just disappeared—never to be seen again."

"Jeepers," Charlie whispered, his voice catching in his throat. "And her father got the job as the lighthouse keeper?"

"Yes," Dickey replied, his eyes narrowing as he looked at his friend. "How'd you know that?"

"It just figures," Charlie replied shrugging. "After all she lived there as a child, didn't she? And there's always been talk around town that she still haunts the lighthouse, right?"

It never ceased to amaze Dickey how fast Charlie could figure something out, even something as creepy as the lighthouse, *and* the story of Eliza Tuffett. "Yeah, right," Dickey agreed somewhat miffed. "They gave up the farm and moved from Mayport to Crystal Falls. As much as

Eliza disliked working on the chicken farm in Mayport, she liked it even less living in a lighthouse."

"She really didn't *live* in the lighthouse," Charlie said correcting him. "She lived in the house *connected* to the lighthouse."

"That's true," he admitted, sighing heavily, annoyed at Charlie's constant interruptions. "Either way," he continued. "The keeper's house doesn't exist anymore because it blew down in the hurricane of 1938." He even surprised himself that he'd remembered the fact about the hurricane that Grandpa had told him. Although his Grandpa was born the year after the killer hurricane, his parent's had told him the stories of the carnage the hurricane had done, and Grandpa in turn passed the stories on. "Anyhow," Dickey continued. "Eliza, having no other choice as a child, grudgingly moved into the keeper's quarters with her parents, went to school here in town, and kept pretty much to herself."

"I can see why she kept to herself," Charlie remarked dryly. "Especially with that big ugly mole on her face."

"Charlie!" Dickey snapped at him angrily, his face turning red.

"Sorry—I didn't mean it," Charlie replied apologetically. "That wasn't nice of me to say. Go on with your story."

"As I was saying," Dickey remarked between clenched teeth, still fuming at Charlie's insensitive remark. "The next year when Eliza was eleven, her mother took ill with some terrible disease. She lost the use of her legs making it impossible for her to climb the winding staircase to the light room in the lighthouse tower."

"Why would she climb up to the tower anyway?" Charlie asked, his forehead scrunched up in wonder. "She'd have no reason to go up there."

"To bring her husband his lunch and dinner when he had to tend to the beacon. You have to remember in those days they actually burned paraffin, or whale oil, inside the refractive beacon lens. They didn't have electricity, so the light produced from whatever source they were burning reflected in the lens. The light was used to guide the ships at sea, and to keep them from running aground on the shoals. The light worked as if the keeper was burning a thousand candles."

"And that's where they got the term candle power from, right?"

"Right," Dickey replied. "Because of her mother's illness, Eliza would carry her father's lunch and dinner to him every day, even coming home early from school to do so. Her journals indicated she spent countless hours with him in the lighthouse, intrigued by the sight of the sea, and how it could change hour by hour. We both know that one time the sea can be calm and serene, glistening in the noonday sun, while the next it can be dark and angry looking if a storm was rolling in." He continued, realizing the sooner he got on with the story, the sooner he could go home. "During their time together her father told Eliza exciting tales of the sea, and about the time he had spent aboard the ships he'd captained. Although I don't know for sure, but from what Grandpa told me, it was her father's stories related in her journals that led her to the sea. Grandpa said it was her destiny, whatever that means." He took a deep breath. "So, the next year, at the age of twelve, she became disenchanted with school, and fed up with living such an isolated life in the lighthouse she left home."

"Don't tell me she went to sea?"

"That's exactly what she did." Another chill ran through him as the evening air turned even cooler. The sun, now a burning fireball, was just beginning to break the fine line of the horizon, and he knew it was getting late. *Time for me to be on my way*, he thought, but he was stuck—stuck telling the tale of Eliza Tuffett. "Eliza left one frigid December night just before Christmas, taking her father's skiff, and rowed across Muffin Bay to the docks. The docks, as her journals mentioned, held a vast amount of ships. There was everything in those days from side-wheelers, steamers and square-riggers bound for San Francisco, South America, the Orient, and other exotic ports of call. Once arriving at the docks, her journals go on to say, she signed on as an able bodied seaman on a trade ship, *disguised as a boy*."

"Holy cow! And no one ever figured out she was a girl?"

"I guess not," Dickey replied shrugging. "Grandpa said her journals referred to her deception of posing as a boy only once or twice. I guess no one on her ship ever picked up on it. Her journals span the difficult years she spent at sea between South America, the Orient, Alaska, and every port in between. They tell of her standing on the stern of a square-rigger in the South Pacific during a full moon watching schools of dolphins swishing through the ship's wake, the moonlight dancing off their skin. They also tell of massive ice floes, brilliant blue in color, drifting silently past the ship when she sailed the unchartered waters of Alaska." Dickey paused and shook his head.

"What?" Charlie asked, his mouth agape. It was obvious he was taken with the tales of her life and wanted to hear more. "What happened to her after her years at sea?"

Dickey looked sternly at him. "We don't have the time to go into that right now. Look," he said pointing to the west. "The sun has almost set, and I've gotta be getting home." Charlie began to protest…and whine as he always did. "I mean it Charlie—I have to go."

Charlie turned and looked at the lighthouse and then turned back, his jaw set. He removed his glasses and rubbed the lenses on his tee shirt. "See the bright light shining in the small window, Dickey? The one you told me about? It just flicked on—just like always—and we're going to go in there tonight!" He leaned forward into Dickey's face. "*And* I want to hear what happened to her after she returned home from her years at sea. Now c'mon, get your bike." Charlie stood and grabbed his bike off the sandy path. "You'll be home before you know it. After all, we're almost at the lighthouse now, and there's no turning back."

Within minutes, they had reached the locked gate of the iron fence surrounding the lighthouse property. They dropped their bikes on the pathway leading to the gate, and stood for a moment staring up at the mammoth-decaying lighthouse. Dickey thought the structure looked even worse in the waning evening light than it did during the day. Its aging paint was badly chipped, and spider web cracks in the concrete walls made it appear that it might simply crumble if he so much as touched it. Four vertical rectangular windows were set directly into the cement edifice, staggered at ten-foot intervals from the base to the top. Two of the windows were high enough, that if he were standing looking out of them, he would be able to see all the way across Muffin Bay to the Atlantic Ocean. One window, about forty feet off the ground, held the brilliant glowing light. The light that had drawn them there—the light they came to investigate—supposedly Eliza Tuffett's guardian beacon.

The beacon in the tower light room flicked periodically, still acting as the guiding beacon for ships at sea. A lighthouse keeper no longer tended the automated light. The keeper had been gone for years, long before Dickey and Charlie were even born. No trespass signs were prominently posted around the perimeter of the iron fence warning anyone breaching the property that they would be duly prosecuted and subsequently fined or imprisoned. The lighthouse and its property were now the responsibility of the United States Coast Guard. It wasn't so much the signs that kept the curious out, but more that it was a well-known fact the lighthouse held a secret. A secret that people only talked about, but no one had the courage to challenge, or for that matter investigate. Least of all Dickey, and least of all tonight.

Dickey's stomach began to roll and grow cold, as if he had swallowed an ice cube. He felt as if he were going to throw up, and yet, as scared as he was to go inside, he didn't want to be the one to back out. If he did, word of his fear would get around like the flu, and by the time school resumed it would be all over town. He was certain if he delayed the inevitable long enough, Charlie would call it quits and the two of them could pedal themselves home and no one would be the wiser. But time was running out, and if Charlie didn't back out soon, the sun would be setting and Dickey would be in big trouble with his parents—big trouble!

"Charlie?" Dickey asked without looking at him, as he stared up at the bright light in the window.

"What?"

"It's really getting late and I should be…"

"Not now," he said interrupting him. "Don't you understand that this is our chance to see if the mystery is really just that, or just some tall tale that's been told over the years to frighten everyone."

"If it is a tall tale, it did a good job," Dickey whispered, unable to take his eyes off the brilliant light in the window. "It scared the dickens out of me."

"What did you say?" Charlie asked as he yanked on the lock to the gate.

"Nothing—I was just thinking out loud."

"Well, do something else besides thinking, will you? See if you can get this lock off the gate."

Dickey held the brass hasp lock in his shaking hand and looked at it. It was evident there was no way the lock would come free without the key. It was one of those hardened steel locks like his father had on his toolbox, and he didn't have to think about it for long. There was just no way the lock was coming off. He let go of it and it clanged noisily against the hasp.

"It's not coming off, Charlie," he said. "Not without the key."

"Then we have no choice," Charlie remarked looking up and down the fence while adjusting his glasses.

Dickey felt a huge sigh of relief come over him. "You mean we have no other choice but to go home?" He asked, turning to pick up his bike.

"Not so fast," Charlie said, his hands gripping the iron bars of the fence as if he were testing its strength. "We'll just scale the fence and get in."

"Are you nuts?" Dickey squealed excitedly, feeling the blood rush to his head. "We can't do that! We could be arrested for trespassing."

"Who's going to arrest us?" Charlie asked, laughing and looking around. "There isn't a soul around here for crying out loud. If there *is* a ghost of that girl inside, she could care less. It's for sure *she's* not going to call the cops. A ghost can't dial a phone!" He let out a loud cackle and before Dickey knew what was happening, Charlie scaled the fence. In a heartbeat he was standing on the other side, smiling, his arms outstretched proving his brashness.

Dickey was dumbstruck and couldn't believe what Charlie had done. His heart was beating like a drum; terrified the police would show up at any moment. In his minds eye he could see the police cruisers rolling up, blue lights flashing, spot lights trained on them with cops piling out, and he and Charlie being led away in handcuffs.

"C'mon!" Charlie said stretching out his arms even higher demonstrating his delight. "We're in! Hop the fence."

Before he knew what he was doing, Dickey was over the fence unsure why he even did it, but he was now on the other side confronting his destiny, and possibly the spirit of Eliza Tuffett.

"What do we do now?" Dickey asked in a shrill whisper. He looked around, his stomach churning, certain that the authorities would appear. But nothing happened. The evening was still with just the hint of a cool breeze, while the night critters chirped their endless songs. The sun had almost set and he was becoming exceedingly nervous about getting home on time. His father's warning rang clearly in his head. *Be home at a reasonable hour.* This was definitely not what he wanted to do.

"Hey," Charlie said grabbing Dickey's attention. "Are you listening to me?"

He hadn't been listening at all. He was too concerned about what might happen if they got caught. "No, I wasn't listening," he admitted. "And I really don't think this is such a good idea."

"Oh come on," Charlie urged tugging at his arm. "Lighten up. Don't be such a wimp!" Playfully he slapped Dickey on the shoulder.

"We're inside the fence now. How bad can it be? Let's go see if we can get inside the lighthouse."

Charlie took off at a dead run heading up the overgrown path leading to the rusted iron door as Dickey followed closely behind still looking over his shoulder. He was certain the police would be pulling up any moment. How could he ever explain it to his parents?

"Dickey—look!" Charlie hollered excitedly as he reached the entrance. "There's no lock on the door!" Without reservation, he yanked back the hasp and with an air of anticipation pulled open the heavy iron door. Dickey was certain the screech of the aging rusty hinges piercing the night would wake the entire town of Crystal Falls. He stood riveted, staring through the open door into utter blackness. Charlie turned and looked at him and then signaled him to come forward.

"Come on," Charlie whispered. "Let's check this place out."

As if in a daze, Dickey walked stiff legged following Charlie closely as they entered the ground floor. Scared of being trapped inside the supposedly haunted lighthouse, and yet unwilling to admit it to Charlie, Dickey grabbed a chunk of loose rock and jammed it under the edge of the door to hold it open. He then stepped inside. It was freezing! He felt as if he'd stepped inside of a tomb. The stench inside the thirty-foot circular concrete first floor was overwhelming, causing Dickey's eyes to water like a faucet. He could hardly catch his breath as he gulped what was left of the cool night air through the open door. The odor was a disgusting mixture of decaying wood and ammonia, and the dampness caused both of them to shiver uncontrollably as they briskly rubbed their arms. It was eerie inside, more so than Dickey had ever imagined, and he found it difficult to speak. Rivulets of moisture seeped down the concrete walls into stagnant pools of water on the floor. They stood motionless inside what appeared to resemble an oversized crypt staring into the darkness and listening. There wasn't a sound, but a tiny sliver of bright light shone from the floor above reflecting on the circular iron staircase. It was apparent the staircase led up into the darkness to the second floor landing, and eventually to the tower light room. As his eyes began adjusting to the dark, Dickey noticed a small wooden table and chair tucked in the corner of the musty room. A leather bound logbook, covered with a heavy layer of years of dust and cobwebs, sat on the table beside what was left of a long extinguished candle. Dickey knew from the stories his grandfather had told that the logbook was something the lighthouse keeper religiously kept of the happenings on his duty shift. It was evident, since the last keeper had left many years ago; the log hadn't been kept since. It lay there abandoned and decaying, much like the inkwell beside it, and not unlike the lighthouse itself.

"What now?" Dickey asked barely able to get the words out of his mouth.

"We climb the staircase and check out the light," Charlie replied matter of factly. "Having the automated beacon in the tower room is one thing," he remarked as if he knew what he was talking about. "But having that bright light burning in one of the windows for no apparent reason is something else altogether." He shoved his glasses up to the bridge of his nose. "We have to check it out! Just think," he said, a peculiar grin crossing his face. "We're probably the only two people in Crystal Falls who've ever had enough courage to come this far."

"I'm not sure I'd call it courage," Dickey replied as another shiver rolled through his skinny body. Charlie looked at him curiously, obviously not comprehending his comment. "What I mean is," Dickey remarked, "Courage might not be a strong enough word for what we're about to do. I'd call it more like we're *nuts*—not courage."

Charlie chuckled under his breath and placed his hand on Dickey's shoulder. "Come on my friend. You and I need to do this. If for no other reason than to prove once and for all there's no such thing as ghosts— especially the ghost of what's her name that supposedly stalks this place."

"Eliza Tuffett," Dickey replied gruffly as he sneaked a peek up the winding staircase. "Don't refer to her as *what's her name*. "Her name is Eliza Tuffett."

"You mean her name *was* Eliza Tuffett—not *is*," Charlie remarked with a huff. "You're getting much too wrapped up in this whole *spirit* thing, Dickey. You're treating her spirit like you know her or something." He gripped Dickey by the shoulders. "Let's not argue about what physical, or metaphysical, state Eliza Tuffett might be in. Let's just go upstairs and check it out."

Dickey despised it when Charlie used big words, especially words he didn't understand. It was difficult for him to argue with Charlie when he wasn't sure he even understood what he was arguing about. He often thought Charlie must've swallowed a dictionary at birth, because he knew words that no one else had ever heard of, and he silently promised himself he'd look up the word, *metaphysical*, when he returned home

"You didn't think to bring the flashlight from the tree house, did you?" Charlie asked in a hushed whisper. Dickey shook his head. Charlie merely shrugged remarking, "no big deal. Let's just go check out this place before it gets any later."

Later? Dickey thought. He shuddered to think how late it might be. He was sure it was close to the time he should be getting home, and here he was inside this forbidden place. Dusk had settled in and yet, they hadn't even climbed the staircase to check out the light. By the time Dickey realized it, Charlie was already on the third step of the winding iron staircase leading to the second level—the level forty feet above the ground floor—the level where the bright light in the window was supposedly shining out across Muffin Bay. Reluctantly Dickey climbed the staircase behind him, his sneakers squeaking loudly on the damp corrugated metal steps, his heart racing, not knowing what to expect once he got there. Moments later, upon reaching the second level, Charlie hesitated motioning with his hand for Dickey to join him. From what Dickey could see in the dim light, the area was smaller than the first floor, and much more confined, emanating a chilling dampness, a feeling that sunk deep into his bones. In one corner was a damaged chair; its lower rungs dangling near the floor. In the far corner, near the lone window, was a moldy deacon's bench. The bench was similar, yet much older and in dire need of repair, to the one Dickey's parents had in the mudroom. It appeared to be at least a hundred years old.

Oh, how I wish I were home instead of here, he thought. He was on the verge of bolting from the lighthouse, but there was no way he was going to cave in and be the first one to run. The bright light near the window cast outlandish shadows that danced eerily on the concrete wall behind them.

"There it is," Charlie whispered hoarsely as he nudged Dickey. "The light."

It was a strange looking light, not like a candle, and certainly not like the tower beacon light. It was brighter, yet smaller and more concentrated, appearing to drift lazily in mid air. And it wasn't set in the window ledge as he had imagined from what his Grandpa had told him. It seemed as if it were floating, not around the room, but rather somewhat stationery as if someone—or something—was holding it in mid air. *Like a spirit!*

"Charlie!" Dickey gasped taking a step back, feeling his mouth go dry. "There's something weird going on here, and I don't know about you, but I'm getting the heck out of here!"

"Don't be silly," he protested loudly, grabbing him tightly by the arm. "We've finally found the light, and now we have to find out why it's here, and as crazy as it sounds, *who* else might be here."

"We *know* why it's here for crying out loud!" Dickey quickly countered. "It's just like my Grandpa said." His breath was coming in short gulps as he tried to make some sense of what he was seeing. "It's the light Eliza's parents set out for her when she left home," he remarked in a hushed whisper. "It's supposed to guide Eliza Tuffett back home."

Before Charlie could answer, a muffled noise—not a loud one—but some sort of metallic clatter caught their attention. It was coming from the floor above them where the beacon was. The two of them stood transfixed, gawking up the winding iron staircase that led to the beacon light room, their faces mirrored in absolute terror. And then they saw it. Whoever, or *whatever* it was, was moving down the iron staircase directly towards them. It was moving slowly, deliberately, somewhat drifting in its movements, appearing like a giant waft of smoke, rather than something human. The figure was clothed in white, its arms outstretched as if it were reaching out for them. It never made a sound as it continued down the staircase heading directly for them. It was no more than ten feet away.

Dickey opened his mouth to scream but nothing came out. He was frozen with fear, scared absolutely stiff, as the *thing*, whatever it was, continued moving towards them. Dickey glanced quickly at Charlie who hadn't moved. Charlie stood riveted to the floor, his arms pinned to his side, and his frightened eyes bulging, as the figure came closer. Instantly, Dickey spun and took off running like he was shot out of a cannon. He bolted down the damp metal staircase, slipping and tripping over his own feet as he neared the bottom. He landed heavily on the concrete first floor knocking the wind out of him. The next thing he knew he was lying on the cold damp floor gasping for breath, as Charlie rushed by him and out the door barely missing stepping on him. Charlie raced by him like he was being chased by the devil himself. Quickly Dickey struggled to his feet, holding his chest and bruised arm, and darted out the door scaling the fence without a second thought. Charlie was already on his bike pedaling like a madman down the dirt path all the while screaming at the top of his lungs. Dickey grabbed his bike and started running with it, in his mind figuring he could make better time on his feet than he could on his bike. He could almost feel the apparition closing in on him. He shot two quick fleeting glances over his shoulder certain *the thing* was gaining on him. His imagination was running wild! Minutes later, once he had cleared the large sand dune near the intersecting paths, he hopped on his bike and pedaled as fast as he could for home. He too was screaming, the desperation in his voice lost in the night. He had never encountered such a thing, and he prayed to God he never would again, if the good Lord would just allow him to make it home safely. Charlie was nowhere to be seen. He was somewhere ahead gobbled up in the darkness. Dickey's mind was racing as he crossed the second bike path, thinking that if he made it home safely, he'd never tempt fate again.

Bobby Page, the consummate class clown, was laughing so hard; he had to sit down on the second floor staircase that led to the lighthouse tower. He couldn't believe he had actually pulled off the greatest stunt of his life, literally scaring the dickens out of his two classmates. Once he regained his composure, he struggled out of the white sheet he had taken from his mother's linen closet. It had afforded him the ghostly appearance he needed to help to pass himself off as the spirit of Eliza Tuffett. The idea of tricking them into believing he was the spirit that haunted the lighthouse came to him on the bus ride home from school a few months earlier. That particular day on the bus, Dickey had related the story of Eliza Tuffett to him, in Charlie's absence, the way his Grandpa had told it to him. He had told Bobby he was going to surprise Charlie at some point by taking him to see the spirit, but for him to keep it a secret between them. At that moment, Bobby knew exactly what he was going to do, but his plan would have to wait until the ideal moment presented itself. If it took months before he could pull it off, he thought, well so be it. It would be worth the wait.

He couldn't believe he had actually fooled Dickey and Charlie with his impression of the young girl's supernatural spirit. "They deserved it!" he happily shouted. "Especially after all the stunts they've pulled on me, and making fun of me for falling asleep in class, and flunking my final math exam. I finally got them!" He cheered gleefully, thrusting his arms in the air in jubilation. He then rolled the sheet into a ball and tucked it under one arm. With his trusty pocketknife he cut the thin shred of clear fishing line that held the miniature votive candle dangling from the ceiling. "The candle worked just as I planned," he murmured as he blew it out. "The fishing line really made it appear as if the candle was floating in space." He descended the staircase to the first floor room and removed the large rock that Dickey had jammed against the open door. Moments later he retrieved his bike from outside the fence at the rear of the lighthouse where he had hidden it from view. "It worked perfect," he announced proudly as he pedaled home chuckling to himself. He was pleased he had finally accomplished what he originally thought was impossible. "Dickey should be more careful what he talks about and who he tells his secrets to."

It had been the timing of the gag that bothered Bobby the most, and the fact of not knowing when Dickey and Charlie were actually going to go to the lighthouse. He knew they would at some point—it was just a matter of time. He had watched for them to make their move as soon as school got out, and then, quite by accident, from one of Dickey's sister's friends, he had heard that Dickey, Kelly, and their parents had gone camping in New Hampshire. If nothing else it gave him time to devise his flawless plan, and to stow his "ghostly" equipment down by the lighthouse. He had been to the lighthouse a number of times, and to his knowledge there had never been any sign of a spirit. As far as he was concerned it was nothing more than a tall tale that Dickey's grandfather had told him to scare him from ever going near the deserted lighthouse. This however, was Bobby's first time inside the lighthouse and it was perfect, just as he had imagined. It had been purely providential that Bobby had happened upon his friends' scheme while in the making.

Returning from a friend's house, Bobby had caught sight of Charlie and Dickey headed down the path that would take them directly to the lighthouse. He had correctly assumed, especially at dusk and heading in that direction, where else could they be going? He had taken off on his bike at lightening speed, cut across the narrow dirt path that led to the marshes and then circled back to the lighthouse. It wasn't the regular bike path, but it would get him to where he needed to go without being detected. The number of large sand dunes as seen from the customary bike paths protected him from being noticed. Stealthily he had climbed to a lookout point on one of the dunes noticing Charlie and Dickey sitting on a boulder talking. Dickey's expression appeared to be one of concern, and Bobby figured correctly that Charlie was trying to convince him to see if Eliza Tuffett's spirit really existed. That was all Bobby needed. Breathlessly he scrambled down the dune. He knew he had only a few minutes to collect his "ghostly" gear he had hidden near the marsh, hide his bike, hop the fence and get inside the lighthouse. He was then ready to give them the shock of their lives. And did he ever! It was definitely worth the wait!

The night air felt good against his face as he turned off the bike path onto the main road. If nothing else, it had been a rewarding night for him, a night when he finally got back at the two of them.

A night he wouldn't forget—nor did he want to—not for a long time.

Dickey spent two long days secluded in the house on punishment, along with the loss of his meager allowance for a week. It was not unexpected because of missing his curfew after promising he'd be home at a reasonable hour. He therefore resigned himself to his punishment and maintained a low profile. He knew better than to challenge his parents' final decision, and trying to explain just what kept him, particularly the spirit of Eliza Tuffett, would be a waste of time. Also not unexpected, after two days in seclusion, was his father suggesting they have a talk, "man-to-man." Reluctantly, Dickey followed his father out to the sun porch nervously taking a seat in the wicker chair facing his Dad. He vividly recalled the incidents when he had been in similar situations. Once in the fourth grade when his grades had slipped dramatically for no apparent reason, and again last year when he and Charlie tried out Charlie's new BB gun, and by mistake shot out a neighbor's window.

His father, Adam, was a person that some people referred to as a "gentle giant." He stood well over six feet tall and tipped the scales at 245 pounds. His demeanor, contradictory to his size, was calm and unassuming. But as reserved as he was, Dickey knew when his father was upset. It was evident by the slight flush in his father's cheeks that he wasn't happy with Dickey—not in the least! Adam's high pressure job of managing multiple training sites on the East Coast for a major cable provider caused him to travel frequently, and the stress took its toll on his home life. He did however; make sacrifices in his work schedule as best he could to attend Dickey and Kelly's extracurricular activities. As a result of his efforts there were very few occasions that he missed.

His father had a distinct and distracting habit, when something was bothering him, of wetting his fingertips and flattening out an errant lock of hair he called a cowlick. It was a clear signal to Dickey that things weren't going to go his way. His father cleared his throat and pulled up a chair opposite him. He had a flushed expression on his face as if his world had just collapsed around him. Dickey fidgeted nervously waiting for his father to speak. He knew whatever was coming wouldn't be good, and he braced himself for the worst.

"Dickey?" His father said calmly, crossing his legs and locking his fingers together around his knee. Dickey didn't say a word. He was waiting for the other shoe to drop. "You realize what you did by coming home later than expected was in direct violation of family rules, don't you?" Dickey was well aware of what he had done, but instead of answering he simply nodded. "Those rules weren't developed in a vacuum," his father continued, wetting down his cowlick again. "The rules are meant for everyone who lives under this roof, not just you and Kelly." He raised an eyebrow expecting an answer.

Dickey nodded again and said, "I realize that, Dad, and I'm sorry I got home late. It was just that we…were kind of…"

"Kind of what?" His father asked his eyes narrowing as he waited patiently.

Dickey fidgeted even more, shifting uncomfortably in the rickety chair. He felt as if he were literally on the proverbial hot seat. "It was kind of like Charlie and me were—"

"Charlie and *I*," His father interrupted, correcting Dickey's use of proper English.

"Yes," Dickey managed to say. "Charlie and *I* were checking out Rocky Neck Lighthouse to see if—"

"*Excuse me*?" His father remarked appearing shocked as he leaned forward in his chair. "You were what?" Before Dickey could answer his father asked. "You were at Rocky Neck Lighthouse?" He slumped back in his chair and rolled his eyes to the ceiling. "Why in heavens name were you at the lighthouse? Don't you realize that even the people who live here in Crystal Falls don't go to the lighthouse?"

"Yes, Dad, I do," he asserted quickly. "But we were checking out the legend of Eliza Tuffett—" He hadn't meant to disclose why he and Charlie were actually at the lighthouse, but the words just fell out of his mouth.

"Eliza Tuffett!" His father repeated incredulous, his voice rising an octave. "Please don't tell me you've been listening to some wild tales your grandfather has been telling you?"

Dickey was stunned! His father had hit the nail on the head. It was evident he was upset—very upset—just by his expression. His father's cheeks flushed even brighter, and it took Dickey a moment to recover. "It was just that Grandpa was telling me about—"

"Oh, I know exactly what Grandpa was telling you about, Dickey," he remarked shaking his head. "I don't know *when* he was telling you those crazy tales, but I do know *what* he was telling you." Dickey sat wide-eyed, staring at his father unwilling to compromise his grandfather's confidence. His father heaved a loud sigh. "Dickey, listen to me, *please*. I've heard the story of that young girl, Eliza Tuffett, and her escapades about her sailing off to the Orient all my life. Actually, if you must know, I first heard the stories about her when I was your age." A long moment passed before he continued, staring deep into Dickey's dark expressive eyes. "Dickey," he said with a troubled squint. "Pay attention to me for a moment while I try to explain." His words were brief and measured. "Don't get me wrong, son. Grandpa means well, and he loves you and Kelly very much. But sometimes, even though he doesn't mean to, he tends to embellish stories he's heard over the years that really have no basis of fact."

Every nerve in Dickey's body was tingling. "But Grandpa told me about Eliza Tuffett's journals, and the bright light in the lighthouse," he countered firmly.

"Please, Dickey!" His father implored holding up his hand. "There is absolutely no evidence, at least to my knowledge, to substantiate the fact that a person by the name of Eliza Tuffett ever existed, or that she ever lived in the lighthouse keeper's residence. And as far as any journals she may have kept, well," he shrugged, "I grew up in Grandpa's house, and I can assure you that I never saw any journals."

"But Grandpa said she lived in—"

"Yes, I know. The keepers house at Rocky Neck Lighthouse," His father remarked shaking his head pessimistically. "And Grandpa also told you her spirit still haunts the lighthouse, right?' Before he could respond his father reached out and took hold of his hand. "Listen, son, trust me. I know what I'm talking about. A lot of what Grandpa told you is simply a tale, nothing more than that. It's more than likely a tale that's been passed down over the generations from his father. No one can prove, or disprove, the stories, and because of that you should take them with a grain of salt."

"But Grandpa said her journals are all stored in his attic."

"Yes, yes, I know. I've heard it all before, but like I said, I've never seen them. As far as I know, and believe me, I don't like to put Grandpa in a bad light, but a lot of this might simply be…in Grandpa's imagination."

"No!" Dickey protested, stiffening in his chair. "I don't believe that, Dad! Grandpa wouldn't lie to me. I just know he wouldn't!"

"I'm not saying he would, son. And he certainly wouldn't tell you a fib intentionally. What I *am* saying is that Grandpa has heard those stories all his life, and he probably believes them after all this time." Dickey sat stunned as his father abruptly stood and stretched his back. "Let's just leave it at that, son, and agree that you should stay away from that lighthouse in the future, okay?" Dickey didn't answer. "I don't want to hear about you going back there again, understand?"

Dickey nodded, disbelieving his grandfather had told him a myth, but he didn't want to challenge his father's wisdom or judgment. Somewhere deep in his soul he knew his father was mistaken—especially since he had been face to face with the spirit in the lighthouse.

"I think we're all set with your punishment, Dickey," his father remarked. "Just remember what I said, okay?" He looked at Dickey waiting for his answer.

Instead of agreeing outright, Dickey frowned for a moment while thinking, and then asked, "Dad? Can I ask you a question?"

"Certainly, son. What is it?"

"Have you ever been to the lighthouse?"

His father appeared stunned by the question, and stammered a bit before answering. "Um, yes, once I think." He replied hesitantly, nervously wetting down his cowlick. Dickey sat looking up at his father, his dark eyes dancing, as an air of anticipation crossed his young freckled face. "But it was a long time ago." His father admitted hastily and softly, as if he'd be overheard.

"When Dad?" He asked, his voice rising with expectation. "When you were a kid?"

His father nodded. "Yes, when I was a kid about your age."

Dickey shifted in his chair again, his pulse racing at the thought that his father may have actually experienced the same phenomena he had. "Tell me about it, Dad," he begged. "What happened? What did you see when you were there?"

His father shook his head averting Dickey's dark searching eyes. "Nothing—I never saw a thing."

"Dad!" Dickey pressed. "Are you sure you never saw anything? I mean, maybe even just a trace of something like a light in the lighthouse window or something? Maybe even a noise, or anything like that?"

"No, Dickey!" He snapped, his expression turning grim as his eyes narrowed into slits. "I told you I saw nothing! Now let's drop it, okay?"

Dickey reluctantly agreed and stood facing his father. Somewhere deep in his gut he knew there was more to the mystery of the lighthouse than met the eye. *And* he was certain there was more to what his father may, or may not have seen when he was a kid. It wasn't that he didn't believe his father; he just had trouble believing his father had told him everything. There was more to it, he thought, and it was up to him to find out what it was. If the spirit of Eliza Tuffett really did exist, and her journals were really in Grandpa's attic, he had to know.

"Are we all set, Dickey?" His father asked.

His question was rhetorical because Dickey knew exactly what his father meant—he meant the conversation was over. "Yes, we're all set, Dad."

"And we understand each other, right?"

"Yes we do."

"Good! Now I'm going to spend some quality time with your mother before dinner. In case you haven't noticed she and I haven't had five minutes to ourselves since I got home because of all this foolishness."

"And you still have your coat and tie on," Dickey observed.

"I do, but not for long," he remarked chuckling, as he stripped off his tie. "Now you must have something to do up in your room, so why don't you run up there and do it. We'll call you and your sister when dinner is ready. And don't forget our little talk."

"Okay, Dad." He turned to leave and then stopped in his tracks. An idea struck him like a bolt of lightening. He had to ask the question. "Dad?"

"What is it?" His father asked preoccupied as he had picked up the evening paper glancing at the front page.

"Is Grandpa coming for the July 4th cookout?"

"I assume so." He replied casually not looking up from the newspaper. "Doesn't he always? Why do you ask?"

"No reason," Dickey shrugged. "Just wondering."

"So what was that all about," Ann Denton asked her husband as she turned the burner off under the steaming kettle.

"It was nothing, honey," he replied cautiously. "Dickey and I were just discussing the merits of keeping your word, and doing what one agrees to do." He took off his jacket and threw it over the chair, and at the same time, in one fluid motion, wet his fingertips and smoothed out his errant cowlick.

"What's the matter?" Ann asked pouring hot water into two large mugs of coffee. "Is everything okay?"

"Oh sure—everything's fine, it's just…"

"Just what?" She asked handing him his coffee mug. "I can tell when something's wrong, Adam, you know that. You have that frustrating habit of wetting down your hair when things aren't right. Is it work?"

"No, not work," he replied shaking his head. "It's Dad, and the stories he's been telling Dickey." They walked into the living room and Adam stood near the fireplace.

"Stories?" Ann asked curiously, as she sunk into the plush easy chair looking concerned. "What kind of stories?"

Adam stared into his mug of coffee for a moment as if he were searching for the answer to the meaning of life. "Stories about Eliza Tuffett," he muttered. "And the mystery of the lighthouse."

"Oh my goodness," Ann gulped appearing shocked as she steadied her mug with both hands. The color literally drained from her face. "You mean Rocky Neck Lighthouse? Why would your father do that?"

"I don't know," he whispered lowering his voice. "But I think I convinced Dickey that the whole thing is nothing more than a figment of Dad's imagination."

"For crying out loud," Ann sighed somewhat relieved. "I certainly hope so. We certainly don't need to relive that all over again."

"Kelly?" Dickey asked poking his head inside his sister's room.

She looked up brushing her blond hair from her face and removing the headset from the CD player. She pushed herself off the bed and sat on the edge. "What is it?" She asked sounding as if he had just interrupted something important.

"I was wondering if I could use your phone for a few minutes."

She looked at him curiously. "Why? Why don't you use the phone in the den downstairs?"

"I...can't. It's kind of...a private call." He was lost as to how to explain his predicament, and even if he could, he didn't want to. "Please Kelly. It's really important."

"Okay," she said with an exasperated tone, and threw the headset on her bed. She let out a long aggravated sigh and rolled her eyes. "Don't stay on the phone long," she ordered just like the older sister she was. "I might be getting a call." Before she closed the door behind her, she said, "And tell Charlie I said hello." She cocked her head back and laughed mockingly.

Her aggravated attitude didn't even make an impact on him since he had more important things on his mind. He picked up the phone and dialed. It rang twice before it was answered.

"Grandpa?" He asked in a loud whisper, barely able to hold the receiver in his sweaty palm.

"Dickey? Is this you?" Grandpa asked, his voice sounding anxious. "Is everything alright? Are Mom and Dad okay? What's wrong?"

"Nothing's wrong, Grandpa," he said quickly, afraid he would frighten him with the phone call. "Everything's fine, Grandpa, and everyone's okay." He sucked in a deep breath trying to steady his nerves. "The reason I'm calling is to see if you're coming for July 4th weekend next week?"

"Of course I am. Don't I always come for the holidays? What's the problem?"

"No problem, Grandpa. I'm just wondering if you could do me a favor when you come?"

"Sure—of course I will if I can. Anything for you my little fisherman. What is it? Don't tell me you want to go out fishing again to the breakwater past Angel Island?"

"No, Grandpa," he replied laughing nervously. "I don't think I'm ready for that again just yet. This is something much more important than going fishing."

"Well then—go ahead young fella, and tell me what could be more important than fishing. What's on your mind?"

Dickey took a deep breath concerned he wouldn't even be able to speak her name. He took a chance and blurted out, "Eliza Tuffett." His voice sounded hollow as he spoke.

An awkward moment of silence followed where neither of them spoke and then Grandpa calmly asked, "What about her?"

"Nothing about *her*, Grandpa. It's about her journals, as you called them. The ones you told me are stored in your attic."

"What about them?" A serious quality crept into his voice. Dickey couldn't remember the last time Grandpa had sounded that serious. There was something in his voice that made Dickey tremble. He had never heard that tone in Grandpa's voice before. He had no choice—he had now opened a door that couldn't be closed—at least not until he found out what he was looking for.

"Do you *really* have her journals, Grandpa?" He crossed his fingers hoping his trust in Grandpa's honesty wouldn't be betrayed.

"Of course I do, Dickey. Why do you ask?"

"Could you bring them when you come for the July 4th holiday?"

Grandpa's attitude immediately changed, and he laughed heartily. "All of them?" He asked sounding surprised. "That's probably not possible, Dickey."

"Not possible, Grandpa? Why not?" A sinking feeling crept into his stomach.

"Well, for one thing, there are too many of them. They go all through her adult life from the age of ten."

Dickey felt the air rush out of him, feeling as though he had failed in his quest, and then he had an idea. "In that case," he asked, "could you just bring just a couple of them when you come?"

Grandpa hesitated a moment and then said, "sure—I guess so. But why are they important? What's your interest in her journals?"

"I…just need to see them—that's all. It's important to me, Grandpa. Do you mind?"

"Of course not, but I still don't understand why. From what I'm hearing in your voice, it seems as if you have another agenda and that's why you're asking? It doesn't sound as if you're asking simply out of curiosity. Are you writing a book or something?

"No Grandpa, I'm not writing a book. You know me; I can't even tell a good story. But it's important that I see her journals."

"Then in that case, no problem, young fella," Grandpa willingly agreed. "I'll pick out a couple of the more interesting ones and bring them along when I come for the holiday. Is there anything else?"

"No. Not really, Grandpa,"

Grandpa chuckled under his breath and asked, "If I were to venture a guess, you want to see them because there's someone who's planted a seed of doubt in your mind about the existence of the spirit of Eliza Tuffett? Someone who's a disbeliever?"

"Well…maybe," Dickey admitted meekly. He shuffled his feet, digging the toes of his sneakers into Kelly's bedroom carpet.

"Is this *disbeliever* anyone I know?" Grandpa asked. A moment passed and then he asked, "Is your father the person who doesn't believe the legend of Eliza Tuffett?" Dickey refused to answer casting his eyes toward the floor. "That's okay," Grandpa remarked. "Even if it is your Dad, we'll prove it to him once and for all."

"Thanks Grandpa," he remarked, his voice choking up. "I really appreciate it. I love you."

"And I love you too," Grandpa replied. "You take care of yourself."

Dickey promised he would and said goodbye. He hung up the phone and pumped his fist in the air. "Yes! At last I'll finally know, and so will everyone else!"

Ann Denton spent most of the morning of July 2nd out shopping for the July 4th holiday, and getting her long auburn hair cut in the style she had always dreamed of, but never had the courage to do. She pulled into the driveway of their home, shut off the van, removed two large bags of groceries and dashed into the kitchen.

In the last few minutes the sky had turned an ominous smokey gray, and she was certain a storm was brewing somewhere in the distance. She immediately abandoned the groceries on the island work counter, figuring the pickles and rolls could wait to be put away, while she closed the windows on the sun porch. She had just closed the second of fourteen windows when her daughter, Kelly, walked in.

"Mom?" Kelly asked startling her mother. "Are you going to take me over to Kristen's house this morning like you said you would? I told Kristen—" She stopped short in her tracks, her mouth agape as she stared speechless at her mother. "Mom!" She gasped. "What did you do?"

"What do you mean, *what did I do*?" Ann asked, hurrying to close the remaining windows just as the rain began. She knew precisely what

Kelly was referring to, but decided not to feed into her daughter's exaggerated horror.

"Your hair, Mom!" She exclaimed rolling her eyes. "Why did you get it cut?"

"Kelly!" Ann said firmly, placing her hands on her hips and facing her daughter. "First of all, I wanted this type of cut all my life, but never had the courage to do it." Lowering her voice and leaning into Kelly she said. "*And* for your information young lady, it wasn't your decision. It was mine, and I like it." Kelly simply shook her head just as Dickey walked onto the porch. "Morning, Dickey," Ann Denton said cheerily. "Are you just getting up?"

"Yes, Mom, I am," he replied and then hesitated for a moment. "Holy cow, Mom!" He exclaimed taking a step back. "You got your hair cut off!"

"Boy!" Kelly exclaimed rolling her eyes in her brother's direction. "You're a quick study!"

"Enough of that bickering you two," Ann quickly chimed in. "Why don't the two of you run out to the van and bring in the rest of the groceries."

Kelly looked aghast at her mother. *"In the rain?"*

"Oh no, certainly not in the rain," Ann replied sarcastically. "I'll drive the van into the kitchen so you don't get wet!" Her terse comment didn't go unnoticed. "Yes, of course in the rain," she replied sharply. "And when you're done I want the two of you to straighten up your rooms, take a shower and get done whatever chores need to be done. I'll have lunch ready soon. Don't forget that Grandpa will be here tomorrow, and we'll have our cookout and go to the fireworks." Neither of them moved. "Go! Scoot!" Ann said brusquely ushering them off the porch.

The rain was coming down in torrents beating steadily on the southwest side of the house and flowing over the gutters. It wouldn't take long, Ann imagined, with the sandy soil of Cape Cod, for the runoff to spill through the miniature cracks in the basement walls and into the cellar. It wouldn't be the first time she and the kids, in Adam's absence, spent the better part of an afternoon vacuuming up the gathering puddles on the basement floor.

"Mom?" Kelly asked as she stumbled into the kitchen dripping wet, with the last of the groceries. She plopped down the two remaining bags next to the ones Dickey had just set on the counter. Dickey took off, bounding up the stairs two at a time, before his mother could ask another favor, as Ann began busily putting away the groceries. "Mother?" Kelly asked again feeling as though her mother had snubbed her.

Ann turned facing her, leaning against the counter. "What is it, Kelly?"

"How come you acted so surprised last night when Dad mentioned to you in the living room about Dickey going to Rocky Neck Lighthouse?"

Ann's eyes narrowed as she stared at her daughter. "I wasn't...surprised," she stammered, lost for words. "You weren't even in the living room when your father and I were talking."

"I know. I...was in the guest bathroom," Kelly admitted sheepishly. "I didn't mean to be listening, it just...happened."

"Well, I won't lie to you, Kelly," Ann managed to say choosing her words carefully. "People don't go to Rocky Neck Lighthouse because it's supposedly haunted." Kelly's eyes widened. "That's all I'm going to say about it, so why don't you just drop the subject and go upstairs and do whatever it is you have to do. And in the future young lady, keep your ears to yourself."

"But, Mom, I—"

"Kelly!" Ann said harshly, her voice rising.

"Okay, okay, I'm going. But it just seems to me there was more to it about the lighthouse than just what I overheard."

"Upstairs, young lady! Now!" Ann turned and faced the stove clasping her hands in front of her to keep them from shaking.

As Kelly reached the second floor landing she saw Dickey standing in the doorway of his bedroom, a look of sheer anticipation on his face.

"I heard you ask Mom about what she and Dad were talking about last night," he whispered. "But I couldn't hear her answer. What did Mom say?"

"You don't want to know," Kelly remarked offhandedly, walking into her room and slamming the door behind her.

The morning of July 3rd dawned hot and dry with Cape Cod devoid of any rain for almost two weeks before yesterday's downpour. Dickey knew it would be a while, even with the recent rain, before he cut the grass again, since the patches of crispy brown turf still crunched under his feet when he walked across the yard. His main concern was, with the exceptionally dry conditions, that the fireworks celebration might be called off. It wouldn't be the first time, and he hoped it wouldn't come to that again. He held out hope that yesterdays storm would be enough not to cancel the festivities. The night before the fourth was one of his favorite holidays with the sky lit up by crackling fireworks resulting in explosions in hues of brilliant colors. The multiple resounding booms of the finale were his favorite part. He loved to count the seconds between the dazzling bursts of color, and when the sound actually reached him. The booming noise always made his chest reverberate, and after the finale he always sat for a few minutes mesmerized, absorbing the grandeur and enormity of the event.

It was well after noon by the time Kelly and Dickey finished their chores and were ready to take their showers to get ready for Grandpa's arrival. Kelly won their legendary, paper, rock, scissors contest they always played to see who'd win the right to take their shower first. As usual, she had won. Minutes later when she had finished, Dickey was in and out of the shower, and furiously drying off when he heard the familiar booming voice of Grandpa coming from downstairs. Dickey's heart leapt at the thought of seeing Eliza Tuffett's journals.

Ten minutes later Dickey entered the living room and was immediately swept into the hulking arms of his grandfather.

"There he is," Grandpa bellowed heartily as he always did. "My big bass catcher! The best fisherman that ever landed on Angel Island!" He wrapped his large arms around Dickey and squeezed him like a rag doll. "For goodness sake!" Grandpa exclaimed, quickly putting him down. "You're getting too big for me to pick up any longer. I'm not as young as I used to be, or," he remarked grinning and ruffling Dickey's hair, "you're not as little as you used to be."

No sooner had he released him, Grandpa looked toward the staircase and his sparkling ice blue eyes danced at the sight of Kelly entering the room.

"Oh my goodness!" Grandpa cried out extending his arms. "There she is! The prettiest girl in Crystal Falls!"

For the next half hour, Grandpa, who had settled himself in the oversized wicker chair on the sun porch, puffed on a pipe full of tobacco while chatting non stop, catching Dickey's parents up on the past few months.

"So," Grandpa said, his typical broad grin spreading across his weathered face as he rubbed his large hands together. "What time do we leave for Wilkins Pond?"

"Not until we have our cookout, just like usual," Ann replied smiling. "And if no one has noticed, I could use some help." Her invitation for help didn't go unnoticed.

As usual, Ann had everything organized on the sideboard harvest table. Adam diligently flipped the burgers, strip steaks and hot dogs on the grill, and acting as the chef, brought the food inside to the sun porch. Macaroni salad, tossed salad, all the condiments, and bags of chips were spread out on the side table. It was truly a Cape Cod summer afternoon culinary delight.

While eating Dickey thought about the upcoming evening at Wilkin's Pond, and couldn't wait for the celebration to begin. Two hours passed while everyone stuffed themselves and then, sufficed, they relaxed and chatted to pass the time as they always did.

Wilkins Pond was the perfect place to watch the fireworks, and over the past years it had become the gathering place for many of the residents of Crystal Falls. The steep side slopes of Wilkin's Pond, and the pine trees covering the hills on the east end of the pond overlooking Muffin Bay, made it the ideal location for the Denton family to view the annual fireworks display. Ann and Adam Denton had packed snacks and drinks for the evening, and after the cookout, sometime before dusk, they'd all pile into the van and head for Wilkins Pond.

"Grandpa?" Dickey asked. "Is Wilkin's Pond what the kids in school call a kettle hole?"

Grandpa thought hard for a moment before answering. "I suppose it is, now that you mention it." He sat back and interlocked his large fingers across his stomach. "Do you even know what a kettle hole is?" Dickey shook his head. Grandpa looked at his son, Adam, and asked, "do you want to tell him?"

"I know what a kettle hole is!" Kelly piped up excitedly before her father could answer.

"Well," Adam said. "Go right ahead honey and tell us."

Dickey glared at his sister thinking, how does she know what a kettle hole is? I'll bet whatever she says a kettle hole is, she'll be wrong. Girls? He thought. They can't even bait their own fishing hooks.

Encouraged to tell her story, Kelly sat upright on the wicker loveseat and began. "A kettle hole is a large depression in the earth that can be as small as a compact car, or as large as a city block. These depressions," she continued barely taking a breath, "were created during the ice age. When the glaciers melted away they left huge blocks of ice that were trapped as the melting water covered them with sand, silt and gravel. Millions of years later when the ice blocks melted the sediment on top created a weight too great to support the land mass and the ground literally collapsed leaving a great depression in the earth. I read that you can tell which ones they are since they generally have steep side slopes, eventually ending up as deep lakes or ponds." She sat back and smiled, obviously pleased with herself.

"Well," her father gushed staring at her as if she had just won the national science fair. "It's nice to know that someone in this family is paying attention in class. Where did you learn about kettle holes?"

"In my earth science class," she replied. And then in a brief, almost imperceptible moment, she turned and stuck her tongue out at Dickey. It was so quick that no one in the room noticed. No one that is except Dickey who simply grimaced.

"So," Grandpa asked picking up his pipe from the end table, "when do we leave for Wilkin's Pond?"

Dickey stared curiously at his grandfather. Had he completely forgotten about Eliza Tuffett's journals? Did he even bring the journals with him? If he had, why hadn't he shown them to him?

Adam looked at his watch. "We probably have an hour or so, Dad, before we have to leave. There's no need to get there too early, unless of course you enjoy being eaten alive by mosquitoes."

"No thanks!" Grandpa said laughing in his own special way. "In that case, I'm just as happy to wait here until it's time to leave."

"Anything I can get for you while we wait, Grandpa?" Ann asked heading for the kitchen.

"Not a thing—thanks! But I could go for a game of dominos if anyone is up for the challenge?" He looked at Kelly and raised his eyebrows. "What do you say?"

"No thanks, Grandpa," she replied indifferently. "I have to call my girlfriend Kristen, and find out if she's going to the fireworks tonight with her parents. We usually meet them at Wilkins's Pond."

"Fair enough," Grandpa replied.

"And don't look at me, Dad," Adam, exclaimed. "I'm going to make a couple of phone calls to the golf course, seeing as we have time before we have to leave."

"Well, look who that leaves?" Grandpa said looking at Dickey and smiling, the creases in his weathered face deepening.

Dickey sat slumped in his chair, staring at his sneakers, his arms folded tightly across his chest. He couldn't believe Grandpa had completely forgotten about the journals—if in fact he had even brought them. Or, as his father had indicated… whether they existed at all.

"Well, whaddaya say, young fella?" Grandpa asked. "Think you can beat me at a game of dominos?" Dickey shrugged without looking up. Everyone had left the sun porch leaving just he and his grandfather. "How about it?" Grandpa asked again.

"Sure—I guess so, Grandpa," Dickey mumbled. He walked over and pulled the box of dominos out of the game chest and without another word, set them up and sat down at the card table. Grandpa sat opposite him and adjusted his jacket and when he did, a brown leather folder fell out and landed on the table.

"Oops!" Grandpa said. "What the devil is this?" He looked at the folder lying on the table and then glanced over his shoulder toward the kitchen. He looked back at Dickey who was sitting in silence staring at the folder. Dickey looked up at Grandpa and his eyes asked it all. "Yes," Grandpa whispered grinning like a Cheshire cat. "I brought a couple of Eliza's journals as you asked. But you have to be quiet about it. I'll bet you thought I had forgotten them didn't you?"

"Oh no!" Dickey steadfastly protested shaking his head. "I knew you wouldn't forget them!" He couldn't bring himself to tell Grandpa the truth that he was beside himself with dismay that Grandpa had actually left home without them. Grandpa looked at him in that special way Dickey had come to know all too well. He knew Grandpa didn't believe him—not for a minute.

"Well, it doesn't matter," Grandpa, said. "What matters is what's in front of you." He tapped his large index finger on the folder. "If you want to read them, you better get going before your folks come back in."

Dickey's trembling fingers opened the worn leather folder revealing a number of aging yellowed pages written in a faded, although exceptionally neat script. It was obvious a young girl had written the journals just by the neat handwriting. He stared intently at the pages trying to make out the words. His eyebrows knitted together as he read.

January 7, 1905. We've been at sea for a little over two weeks, and I haven't been seasick yet. The work is difficult and the food is not good. We have ground cornmeal mash twice a day, along with water and citrus fruit. Fruit is good, the captain says because it helps to prevent rickets and scurvy. I'm careful when I use the head that no one notices I'm a girl. So far, so good, nobody has noticed yet. The weather is calm and getting warmer as we sail south. I wonder if I'll ever get over the wonderful feeling of such freedom when I stand on the deck at night during a full moon and watch the sails snapping in the wind? We're currently off the coast of southern Florida near the Florida Keys. I had to repair the jib this morning, since it was torn in the storm we hit off

South Carolina. The first mate said I did a good job. Hope my good luck holds out. I have to go now journal. I'll write more later.

Dickey was awestruck and couldn't believe he was actually reading Eliza's diary. He flipped through a few more pages and then something caught his eye. It was a reference to Rocky Neck Lighthouse.

April 2, 1905 – Weather is finally clearing. Warm and windy today, and the sails are full. Captain says we're somewhere off the coast of Buenos Aires. Our hold is full of wheat, grain and barley. We hit a bad storm over the last three days, many of the men are sick, and the ship smells terrible. I broke three fingers on my left hand two days ago when an accident in the lashing lines on deck caught them. They're taped up now and seem to be okay. Best news I got was when we were in Argentina near the Straight of Magellan where we were given shore leave. Beautiful town where we docked. People are sweet and gentle. Some of the crew got drunk on rum while on shore leave, and it was very noisy that night in our sleeping quarters. As a result I didn't sleep a wink. I didn't stay that long on shore leave because I was afraid I'd be found out as a girl, but I heard all the stories of what went on. Received a long letter from my parents dated back in February. Took three months for it to get to me. I was surprised they said they've placed a vigil light in one of the windows of Rocky Neck Lighthouse as a guiding light for my safe return. Still not sure if I'm going back home when I'm finished with this trip. We're on to our next stop tomorrow morning, which from what I've heard from the

scuttlebutt is Lima, Peru. It should take us about a week or more,
depending on the trade winds, to get there around Cape Horn. I hope
time passes quickly as I'm looking forward to getting to the Orient. I've
heard so much about the people and the food. The one thing I want to see
is a Sampan—but I don't know why? I guess it's just because they look so
interesting in the picture books. Got to go now journal, lots of work on
deck to be done, and I'm a deck crew worker. Have to close for now, I'll
write more later.

Dickey closed the file and looked at Grandpa, unable to speak.

"Satisfied?" Grandpa asked smiling. He reached out and picked up the journals jamming them inside the leather folder and tucked it back in his pocket.

Dickey could only nod. The journals were more than he had ever imagined. As far as he was concerned the journals were indeed authentic, and Grandpa had proved it.

Now the trick would be to see if he could convince his father to join he and Charlie at the lighthouse to finally prove the existence of the spirit of Eliza Tuffett. After all, he and Charlie had seen her, and as frightened as he was that night, it was important that he convince his father.

That in itself, he mused, would be a challenge.

In his subtle and thoughtful manner, Grandpa pulled Dickey aside while at the fireworks display cautioning him about making a snap judgment, and persuading him to relax, and count to ten. His suggestion to Dickey that he sleep on his excitement about the discovery of Eliza's journals was advice well taken. *Especially,* Grandpa said, before Dickey approaches his father about accompanying Charlie and him to investigate the mystery of Rocky Neck Lighthouse.

Generally Grandpa didn't stay overnight after a holiday visit, but since it was late and it had been a long day he thought better of making the long drive home.

And guess whose bedroom was chosen as the guest room for Grandpa? Dickey could count on one hand the number of times Grandpa had stayed overnight, but he was always glad when he did, even if it meant giving up his room. He wished however, that Grandpa would ask to stay in Kelly's room just once.

Reluctantly, and with a scowl on his face rivaling the size of Mount Rushmore, Dickey threw his sleeping bag and pillow down on the floor of Kelly's bedroom.

She glanced at him never moving from her computer and remarked. "It looks like Grandpa is staying the night." Her remark was accompanied with a wry grin, knowing just how much Dickey intensely disliked sharing her room—for whatever reason. She let out a faint, deriding chuckle, as she returned to her computer. "I'll bet you're glad it's just for one night," she mumbled under her breath.

"Look, Kelly!" Dickey snapped. "I'm not happy about this sleeping arrangement either if you must know. But it's worth it just to have Grandpa spend the night."

There was no way he could let on to her why it was so important that Grandpa stay overnight. Grandpa's assistance with the evidence of Eliza's journals was essential for Dickey to gain his father's support. He turned back to his sister. "Are you sure you don't want to tell me what you and Mom were talking about downstairs about the lighthouse?"

"I'm sure," she replied firmly without looking up.

He disliked it when she wouldn't fight with him. If she would, he imagined, at least he'd have the advantage of being able to yell louder than she. It was useless, he thought. He might just as well go to sleep and forget it.

The next morning dawned bright and clear, as Dickey walked into the kitchen confronting his grandfather who was sipping coffee from his favorite mug. It was the mug Dickey had given Grandpa on his 60th birthday. Grandpa had purposely left it at Dickey's house so he could use it when he visited.

"Good morning, young man," Grandpa said. "You want some breakfast?"

"Sure—Grandpa, thanks," he replied sitting down at the table. "You want some too?"

"I had my breakfast a long time ago," he replied chuckling. "If I slept in as late as you, your discussion with your dad would never take place. I'm pleased you took my advice and slept on your decision before speaking with him." A distant gaze passed across his face and then he ran his fingers through his beard and winked. "Your Dad's out on the sun porch, and I'd say this is about as good a time as any to speak with him."

Dickey's hands were clammy as he tried to imagine how to approach the subject with his father. His father's words of warning still rattled in his head. *Don't go back there again.* Finishing his bowl of cereal he stood, riveted in place as if his sneakers were nailed to the floor. *What would his father say? What if his father just told him to forget about anything to do with Rocky Neck Lighthouse?*

"Well?" Grandpa said snapping Dickey from his trance. "Remember, it was you who wanted this moment with your Dad. It was your curiosity about Eliza's journals that's brought you this far."

"I know," he replied nodding numbly, as he looked into his grandfather's sparkling blue eyes. He took a deep breath and asked, "are you coming with me to meet with Dad like you said?"

"No, not this time," he replied shaking his head and placing his large hand on Dickey's shoulder. "I hope you understand, but this is *your* journey, Dickey, and every man has to chart his own course. I did tell you I'd support you, and I have, particularly by letting you read some of Eliza's journals, but now it's time for me to go."

"Go?" Dickey asked the words catching in his throat. "But what about…"

"I've already said my goodbyes to your sister and to your parents. I was just waiting for you to come downstairs."

Dickey rushed into his grandfather's arms wrapping his arms around his waist. It was all he could do to keep from crying right on the spot.

"But Grandpa!" He exclaimed on the verge of tears. "There's so much I haven't told you! There's something very important I need to share with you. Something from last year when we were stranded together on Angel Island."

"Whatever it is," Grandpa said peeling Dickey's hands from around his waist. "I'm sure it can wait until we get together the next time—maybe over the Labor Day weekend. You have enough to deal with at the moment without worrying about something else, no matter how important you think it might be. What you're dealing with right now is much more important, trust me. I did as you asked," he said tucking the leather folder that held Eliza's journals under his arm. "Now it's time for you to take care of your end of the deal." Grandpa hugged him tightly and kissed him gently on the top of his head. "Now go," he whispered holding Dickey's freckled face in his large rough hands. "Like I said," he whispered with a quick wink. "It's your journey, young fella, and it'll be a journey you won't soon forget."

Then before Dickey could even take a breath, Grandpa was gone out the side door into the breezeway. He watched as Grandpa's red short bed pickup truck backed out of the driveway and moved slowly down the street. He stood there watching as the truck turned the corner and disappeared from sight. His breath left him and he felt lightheaded as the room became eerily quiet except for the loud thumping of his heart.

"What did Grandpa mean by a journey you won't soon forget?" he wondered aloud. His spell was broken by the sound of his father's voice calling him from the sun porch. He felt like running as fast as he could—somewhere—anywhere! In many ways he felt he wished he'd never heard of—or better yet—never had seen the spirit of Eliza Tuffett. "Girls!" He mumbled aloud. "Spirits or real, I'll just never understand them!"

"Dickey!" His father called out again. "Did you hear me?"

"Yes Dad, I'm coming." It was all he could do to make his body move in the right direction. Walking out onto the porch he was surprised to see Kelly and his mother, as well as his father. It was apparent his sister and mother had strategically positioned themselves in a way they couldn't be seen from the kitchen. He stopped short and all thoughts of discussing the existence of the spirit of Eliza left his mind. The presence of the rest of his family, their eyes fixed on him made him feel as if he was on the carpet for violating some important family rule. It appeared to him as if the jury had already made up their minds, and had decided on the appropriate punishment. He took a deep breath, wiping his sweaty palms on his camouflaged shorts.

"Have a seat," his father said in a calm controlled voice pointing to the nearest wicker chair. He didn't sound upset—*concerned*—but not upset. His father wet his fingertips and smoothed out his wayward cowlick. "First of all, Dickey, you've done nothing wrong, so let that statement set the tone for this family meeting." He arched his eyebrows in anticipation of an answer.

"Okay," Dickey replied, lost for words as he sat down. Even his slight build caused the interwoven strips of wood in the wicker chair to groan. How he wished Grandpa had stayed to help him defend his argument of the existence of Eliza's spirit, and her journals. He swallowed, clearing the lump in his throat. "If nothing is wrong…then why is everybody here?" His eyes shifted nervously around the room between his parents and Kelly. Something peculiar was going on. He could feel it in his gut.

His father sat back and quickly glanced at Dickey's mother. "Do you want to start, Ann?"

She nervously cleared her throat and nodded. "Sure…I guess so." She shifted in her chair as Kelly looked at her expectantly. "What I'm going to tell you, Dickey," his mother said glancing quickly at Kelly, "and to you, Kelly, might be a little hard for the two of you to understand, but I'll try my best." She rolled her eyes toward the ceiling and took a deep breath, trying to compose herself. "I told this to Kelly earlier," Ann admitted to Dickey, "after she overheard a conversation between your dad and me the other night. Not to frighten you, but Rocky Neck Lighthouse is…indeed haunted." She settled back exhaling deeply.

"By the spirit of Eliza Tuffett?" Dickey blurted out, his eyes growing wide.

"Please, Dickey!" his father said, admonishing him for interrupting. "Let your mother finish."

"Sorry," Dickey mumbled, glancing briefly at Kelly whose expression remained impassive.

"Anyway," Ann continued. "As I was about to say, I heard all the stories about the haunted lighthouse when I was a young girl in the early 70's. None of us kids really believed the tales then, but we also never had the courage to investigate the spirit that supposedly haunts the lighthouse.

And there aren't any facts to prove that a spirit really exists. In either case, investigating it just wasn't the thing to do."

"So you just stayed clear of the lighthouse?" Kelly interrupted looking at her mother.

Ann nodded. "Yes we did, as most of the residents of Crystal Falls have done for generations."

"Well, I don't believe it," Dickey remarked, his voice nervously cracking, as he sat up straight in his chair.

"Don't believe what?" His mother asked, her brow furrowing. "You don't believe people have stayed clear of going there for generations?"

"No. It's not that," Dickey remarked. "It's just that I believe the lighthouse really *is* haunted." He couldn't believe he had actually spoken the words. "I mean—"

"You mean what?" His father asked leaning forward in his chair. Dickey fidgeted nervously, the wicker chair squeaking wildly. "Son? What do you mean, you believe it is really haunted? Why would you say such a thing?" A long moment of silence followed.

"He doesn't know what he's talking about," Kelly remarked sardonically.

"Yes, I do!" Dickey insisted. He looked at his father. "You've gotta believe me—I really do know what I'm talking about!"

"Okay, okay, settle down, son," Adam remarked. "We're just here to…I guess you'd say, clue you and Kelly in on a little unknown piece of history regarding our family." His father shifted in his seat. "Now tell us why you believe that a spirit really exists at the lighthouse?"

Dickey's dark eyes darted between his parents and Kelly, trying to think quickly as to how to explain the mystery that he and Charlie had encountered.

"He has no idea," Kelly remarked skeptically letting out an exaggerated sigh. "He's just talking for the sake of talking."

"Kelly! Please!" Her father said glaring at her, and then turned back to Dickey. "Go ahead, son, tell us why you believe there really is a spirit?"

"Be…because we saw it…her."

"*We* saw her?" Adam asked his brow furrowing into deep irregular rows. "*We who*?"

"Me and Charlie Sullivan," Dickey replied lowering his eyes. "I probably should've told you sooner, but I didn't think it was a big deal, until…"

"Until what?"

"Until we actually saw her spirit when we were inside the lighthouse, and she scared the daylights out of us. We couldn't pedal home fast enough. I was so scared I fell down the stairs from the second floor and got the wind knocked out of me. Charlie just about ran over me trying to get out of there."

Kelly was now enthralled, her attitude visibly changing as she stared at her brother.

"Tell me about your experience." His father asked evenly, wetting his fingertips and smoothing down his cowlick. "What happened, son?"

Dickey took a deep breath, believing his heart might leap out of his chest. "We snuck into the lighthouse and climbed to the second level where we saw the light that everyone talks about, but it wasn't in the window like everyone says. It was kind of floating in mid air."

"Go on." His father pressed.

Dickey felt the blood rush to his head, wiping his palms on his shorts for what seemed like the hundredth time. "And then the ghost...or spirit, or whatever you call it, came down the stairs with its arms outstretched like it was going to capture and kill us!"

"Okay, okay, calm down, Dickey," his father said holding up his hand. "First of all I suspect that you and your friend, Charlie, have been tricked by someone trying to make you believe you actually confronted the spirit of Eliza Tuffett." Dickey was stunned. After all, he'd seen the spirit, along with her journals that his grandfather had shared with him. He opened his mouth to speak but nothing came out. His father shook his head and continued. "Trust me, Dickey, someone is pulling your leg. I suspect it's nothing more than a cruel joke that's been played on you."

"But Dad!" Dickey protested. "I saw her journals, and I know she exists—I know she does!"

His mother looked aghast, her jaw slackened as she stared at Dickey. Kelly's head swiveled between her mother and Dickey trying to comprehend the enormity of the situation.

"You saw her journals?" His father asked in a composed manner, while moving forward in his seat. "Tell me you're kidding."

"I'm not kidding, Dad," Dickey pleaded. "I promise—I saw them! Grandpa showed them to me. I read them just yesterday when he was here. If they're real, then she, or at least her spirit, must be just as real."

Adam glanced at his wife—who appeared visibly shaken, blankly staring back at him—obviously lost for words.

Adam looked back at his son. "Do you remember what the journals said, son?"

"Yes." His breath was now coming in short bursts. "They talked about her voyage to South America around Cape Horn and other things, like how she broke three fingers when they got caught in the lashing lines on deck."

"Oh my Goodness!" Ann gasped holding her hand to her mouth.

"What is it, Mom?" Kelly asked, appearing frightened at her mother's reaction to her brother's recollection. "What haven't you told us?" She placed her hand on her mother's forearm. "Dad said something earlier about how this was part of our family history."

Adam sank back in his chair and rubbed his forehead glancing furtively at his wife.

Ann shook her head and then looked at her husband. "It's *your* family history, Adam," she stated assertively. "I'd suggest *you* begin."

Kelly and Dickey sat silent, barely breathing, their eyes fixed on their father waiting for him to speak.

Adam interlocked his fingers in a tight fist and placed them in his lap. "It's important, children, at least in your mother and my eyes, that you know the truth about the secret of the lighthouse, and how it involves our family."

So, this is what Grandpa meant, Dickey thought, about a journey I won't soon forget.

Ann Denton sat silent on the loveseat beside Kelly, as Adam spoke to the children. Ann's expression was painfully drawn as if she had been through a terrible ordeal and was just recovering. Kelly, even for her age, was intuitive enough to perceive that something wasn't right. Her mother's typical strong constitution and sense of humor had all but vanished.

"Mom? Are you okay?" Kelly asked, chewing nervously on her lower lip while staring at her mother. "You look like you've seen a ghost."

Ann closed her eyes and shook her head. "I'm fine, Kelly," she whispered opening her eyes and looking at her husband. "Please Adam," she asked. "Go on and finish your story."

Adam inhaled deeply, nervously rubbing his hands on his knees. "Where do I begin?" He mumbled more to himself than to the others.

"At the beginning," Ann said answering his question. "Please!"

He could tell that his wife was beginning to lose control of her emotions, and if he was to be honest and forthright with the children, he knew he had to start now.

"Eliza Tuffett," Adam began, "as you're all well aware by now, was born in 1892, right here in Crystal Falls." He looked guardedly at Dickey and Kelly. "Bear with me for a moment, because what I'm about to tell you is important. It's not something I can just jump into the middle of and expect you to make any sense of the whole thing." He paused waiting for their reaction, and when there was none he continued. "Eliza's younger years were fairly uneventful, especially since she was an only child. She attended grade school here in town and performed only marginally. She wasn't a great student, but not the worst one either. She was more of a bookworm and a dreamer, rather than performing as a good student." He paused and looked at Kelly. "Your middle school is named what?" He asked. Kelly appeared confused by his question. She glanced at her mother and then looked back at her father.

"You know the name of my school, Dad," she replied. "It's the Josiah Wheeler Middle School."

"Yes," Adam replied. "Yes it is. And it's named after the famous whaling ship captain, Josiah Wheeler, who one could say, just about founded this town. Josiah Wheeler essentially put this town on the Cape Cod map and was the richest man in the county. He built that 14-room mansion, the one down by Muffin Bay, at a cost of over five hundred thousand dollars. I would venture a guess that by today's standards it would cost about ten million dollars."

"Dad," Kelly said sucking in her breath interrupting him. "Please don't get me wrong, and I don't mean to be rude, but is there a point to all of this?"

"Yes, honey there is," he replied dryly. "Your school as you know it today, although it's named after Josiah Wheeler, wasn't built until the early 1960's. But it was built on the same footprint as the original school by the same name that was built in 1870, and burned down in the late 1950's. The original school was the school Eliza Tuffett attended."

"Not for long," Kelly remarked, and then just as quickly she explained her statement. "What I mean, Dad, is, if she left home when she was twelve, she couldn't have attended middle school for all that long."

Her father nodded. "I agree—you're right, but that's beside the point. The point is that you are living a little piece of history just by attending that school. After all, both your mother and I went there, and Dickey will be going there next year."

"Adam, please!" Ann managed to say, rolling her eyes. "Get to the point."

"Yes, sorry," Adam said holding up his hands, palms out. "I didn't mean to digress. I just thought it was important they understand the history, that's all."

"Well, it isn't that important, Adam!" Ann remarked tersely. "At least not as far as the children are concerned. That's ancient history—not family history. Please just continue."

"Dad?" Dickey said interrupting his mother. "I guess I don't understand whatever happened to Eliza, and why Grandpa has her journals?"

Kelly broke in glaring hard at her brother. "Let Dad finish for crying out loud!"

"I am! I'm just asking the question." Dickey had the greatest urge to stick his tongue out at his sister, but refrained, since he knew he'd be caught and punished.

"Let me go into the story," Ann remarked. "It might be easier if I tell you the story, rather than your father. He's a little too close to the situation to be objective. I'll tell you the details; but you have to be patient." Dickey and Kelly turned and looked at her, expressions of anticipation crossing their young anxious faces. "Whatever you may have read of Eliza's journals, Dickey," Ann began, "which I must say, Grandpa really had no right to share with you, are probably fairly accurate. What you *don't* know is what really happened to her during, or after her journey."

Dickey shifted again in his squeaky wicker chair, feeling as if his world was falling apart around him. He had seen the real writing of her journals and truly believed them, and he had seen her spirit walking the lighthouse.

Ann placed her fingertips on her temples, as if she was trying to recall the actual events through mental telepathy, or she had a splitting headache.

"It's true," Ann eventually said. "Eliza did take her father's skiff from the dock that frigid night, sometime shortly before Christmas Eve in 1904. And she did, Dickey, as I assume you read in her journals, sail to South America." Ann paused. "Exactly what journals of hers did you read?"

"Um," he stammered feeling the pressure. Although he didn't dare look at his father, or Kelly, he could feel their eyes boring holes through him. His voice sounded distant and small in his own mind as he answered. "What I read," he finally said in a hollow tiny voice, "were the parts about her trip around Cape Horn after passing Buenos Aires, and then going on shore leave in Argentina." He took a breath feeling as if someone had let the air out of him. "Her journals also mentioned how she had to be careful not to be found out as a girl while on shore leave."

His mother nodded and asked. "And then what?"

"And then her journal mentioned that she received a letter from her parents, dated three months earlier, telling her they had placed a light in the window of Rocky Neck Lighthouse as a symbol for her safe return." He took another deep breath, surprised at how much he could recall, especially under stress. "The journals then mentioned about her going on to Lima, Peru, California, the South Pacific, and to the Orient to see a Sampan." His forehead knitted for a moment and he remarked, "I don't even think I know what a Sampan is?"

"It's a boat, for crying out loud!" Kelly butted in.

Ann acknowledged Kelly's statement, and then looked back at Dickey. "That was after the accident Eliza suffered, was it not?"

"Yes Mother," he replied keeping his eyes fixed on her. "From what she had written it seems it was sometime after she broke her fingers in some lashing lines on deck before arriving in Peru."

"As it happens," Ann said, "Lima, Peru, turned out to be not the best port in the world for her, since she became extremely ill while there from some sort of rare parasitic disease. She was sick for weeks during the remainder of the trip to California, and it took its toll on her body, causing violent stomach cramps, loss of body fluids and high fevers. Most of the time she spent confined to her quarters in a state of delirium. And all the while she had to cover up the fact that she was a young girl—not a boy. You have to remember, conditions and life on board a working trade ship in those days, a hundred years ago, was unlike anything we could ever imagine. The food was marginally nutritious at best, and the crews living quarters were, well…deplorable. It wasn't uncommon for their quarters to be infested with rodents and insects. It's been written that the odor below decks would take a strong man's breath away. So, that being said, imagine yourselves trapped in bleak, dank living quarters below decks, with terrible food, the place rampant with rodents, and all the while you're suffering from a severe ailment such as she was."

"But why didn't the doctor on the ship help get her well?" Dickey asked.

Ann smiled at his innocence. "In those days, the presence of a real doctor was pretty much reserved for the grand sailing ships who had paying customers—not for the poor unfortunate souls who were working on trade ships."

"That's terribly unfair," Kelly remarked.

Ann shrugged indifferently. "Yes, it is, but that's the way life was in those days. If one of the crew died from disease, or an accident, they'd just get another man from a tavern in another town who was looking for work, or was running from the law."

"That's so sad," Kelly remarked again. "Everyone deserves good medical care no matter who they are."

"That's true," Ann agreed. "But like I said, things were different a hundred years ago. There weren't any child labor laws, and so long as a person could walk and breathe, they'd be hired. The next best thing to a ship's doctor was what they called the ship's pharmacist. He was actually called an alchemist in those days. The big drug of the day was opium, and they used it for everything from a toothache to appendicitis. The alchemist heavily medicated Eliza, and six weeks later once they arrived in California, he tried to get her to stay in San Diego and go to a hospital. But in the end she refused because she couldn't risk having them find out she was a girl. If they had, they would've put her on the first stagecoach back home, and she would've lived out her remaining years in misery knowing she had never accomplished her goals."

"What happened to her then, Mom?" Kelly asked, caught up in the excitement of the story. "I mean what happened to her once they reached California if she didn't go the hospital?"

"Miraculously she got better, gaining back a lot of her strength, and after a week in port she was strong enough to perform her duties, and a month later continue on to the South Pacific. The captain however wanted her off the ship because he thought she couldn't handle her duties after her illness, but still didn't know she was a girl. I think he may have thought of her as a jinx as well. People in those days were big into superstition and jinx's, and all they needed was an excuse."

"So what happened, Mom?" Dickey asked.

"That's where her story gets interesting," Ann remarked. "The first mate was a hardy young fellow from Boston, named Luke. Eliza's journals mentioned the fateful day her disguise as a boy was finally discovered. They were two days out of San Diego when she and Luke were alone on the deck splicing lines and a freak storm came up and blew off her sailor's cap. She knew immediately what happened when she felt a lock of hair brush her forehead. Her notes said that Luke appeared instantly dumfounded. It was at that moment he realized she was a girl. Because he cared for her, he swore he'd never tell the captain or the crew, and from that day on their relationship blossomed into love. Luke had plenty of sea experience, having gone to sea when he was fifteen working as a deck hand up and down the East Coast. He was a few years older than Eliza and stuck up for her. He even went so far as to go to the captain and plead her case, defending her ability to pull her own weight. The captain finally relented, although reluctantly, and kept her on, but criticized her work every chance he got."

"What a bum!" Dickey growled. "He was lucky to have her."

"Yes, he was," Adam, replied agreeing. "Very lucky to have her, but let your mother finish the story."

"A month later," Ann continued, "after taking on provisions in San Diego, the ship sailed off to Micronesia and spent ten months in the South Pacific, and then, after visiting and trading on other islands, sailed on to the Orient. It was a tough six week voyage however, and they ran into a number of severe storms including a typhoon."

"A what?" Dickey asked. He had never heard that word before.

Before his mother could answer, Kelly piped up. "A typhoon. It's like a hurricane except it occurs over water, in this case, over the ocean."

"Well," Adam remarked. "Between being a walking book of knowledge on kettle holes, and now on typhoons, you should sail right into high school next year."

Kelly grinned, sitting up straighter in her chair, proud of his compliment. "Thanks, Dad."

Dickey overlooked Kelly's apparent arrogance asking, "was Eliza okay in the storms, Mom? Did anything happen to her?"

"No, nothing happened to her," his mother answered, a smile creasing her lips.

"What is it, Mom?" Dickey asked. "Why are you smiling?"

"I was just thinking about something funny that happened while she was in the South Pacific."

"Tell us, Mom," Dickey urged shifting forward in the wicker chair.

"One time," his mother began, "on one of the smaller islands that Eliza and her crew landed on in Micronesia, long before she arrived in the Orient, she adopted a native monkey. Her journals claimed he was a cute little fella that she named Luke, after the first mate she liked so much. I guess you could say her friend Luke, the man, not the monkey, gave her a new lease on life, and it was fortunate they had met."

"Did she eventually made it to the Orient?" Dickey asked.

"Oh yes, she did," Ann said. "Months later however, and not without a great deal of turmoil. Two of the crew on her ship were lost in a giant storm in the South China Sea, and a half dozen others succumbed to scarlet fever. Her journals recounted the events of their burials at sea long before they reached Singapore."

"I can't believe you know so much about Eliza, and what happened to her!" Dickey exclaimed. "You've obviously read her journals, which I didn't know."

Ann glanced quickly at Adam, and then returned her attention to the children. "While in the Orient," Ann continued, overlooking Dickey's comment about the journals, "Eliza was quite taken with the Chinese people, their culture, and their customs. You have to remember," Ann said, "Eliza was in a place and time a hundred years ago when things were much different than they are today. She felt so bad for one little girl near the side of a road; she went back to the ship and returned giving the girl Luke, the monkey, as a gift. The people in those days were restrained by a monarchy, and living under a warlord, who controlled their minds and their beliefs. And yet, through it all, she found her adventure nothing less than fascinating." Ann paused and lowered her eyes.

Dickey looked at Kelly and then to his father before turning his attention back to his mother.

"What is it, Mom?" He asked. "What's the matter?" Ann shook her head and didn't answer. "Dad?" Dickey asked looking at his father.

"Its better that your mother continue with the story." His father's brief reply was all Dickey needed to know not to ask him again.

"Mom?" Dickey asked more assertively than he thought he could. He wasn't one for confrontation, especially with his parents, but this was different. He had to know. "Mom, please. Don't leave me and Kelly hanging?"

Ann relented. "It seems that Eliza ran into some kind of trouble while her ship was in Singapore about a month after they tied up. She was a week short of her fourteenth birthday by then, when she was arrested for stealing something of absolutely no value or significance whatsoever from an outdoor street market. The authorities could never prove conclusively it was she who was the thief, but they threw the book at her anyway and took her before some trumped up tribunal court. They sentenced her to thirty years in prison."

"Thirty years?" Dickey whispered incredulous, as Kelly sat mute, looking shocked, staring blankly at her mother. "How could they do that to her?" Dickey asked. "She was just a kid, no older than me and Kelly."

"Like I said," Ann replied. "It was a hundred years ago, and anything was possible in those days. Remember, there were no civil rights, as we know them today. Anyway," she said, straightening in her chair and appearing more relaxed, "all was not lost." Dickey breathed a sign of relief expecting some good news, and wiggled to the edge of the squeaky wicker chair. "She ended up spending only three years in the infamous

Chinese penal complex called Shai Gai Prison, which as I recall was somewhere north of Shanghai. It took a terrible toll on her and she lost over 30 pounds while incarcerated. The conditions and food were dreadful, and she suffered repeated beatings from the sadistic guards, but she never confessed to the crime. Her cell was nothing more than a six by eight concrete chamber with no window and a mattress made of straw…"

Kelly shivered at the thought of the indecencies Eliza must have endured, and asked her mother to continue without going into the distasteful details.

"Eliza maintained her innocence all the while she was imprisoned," Ann continued. "No matter how bad things got for her, she wouldn't bend."

"Good for her!" Dickey exclaimed, feeling as if he was hearing a fictional story, but knowing it was true. "She must have had a very strong will. But I guess I don't understand why she only spent three years in prison when she had been sentenced to thirty years? From what you've told us, it doesn't seem like her captors would be that kind to shorten her sentence?"

"Because the court," Ann explained, "for whatever reason, knowing full well she was a girl, determined if they allowed her to get married and give birth to a son, they would reduce her sentence to time served and release her. Their culture is very much into the male species, and that's why they made such a deal. My belief is the prison officials were disappointed they couldn't break her spirit, emotionally or physically, and it was better for them to have her out of there as quickly as possible. She was more trouble than she was worth. The longer she stayed there with her defiant attitude, the more strength and conviction she displayed to the other prisoners."

"But how could she be married and have a baby while in prison?" Kelly asked. "From what you told us, she wasn't even engaged to anyone? Not only that, her ship would've sailed long ago while she was locked up in prison, and there was no one left she knew to…save her, least of all to marry her and get her…pregnant?"

Ann chewed nervously on the inside of her cheek, first locking eyes with Dickey and then Kelly. It was apparent to Ann by Kelly's question that she had a sneaking suspicion of what she was about to say. *It's no use*, Ann thought, imagining that she might as well be honest and up front with both of them.

"Her friend, Luke," Ann whispered, "never put out to sea when their ship left port in Singapore. He stayed on in the city and worked at numerous odd jobs to support himself while Eliza was in prison. He would visit her as often as he could, or was allowed. He was heartsick at her predicament and promised he'd care for her as much as possible under the harsh conditions. He was the only person in her life that made any sense to her, and because of his devotion, and love for her, she somehow survived."

"What was he like, Mom?" Kelly asked, her tone tempered. "Was he handsome and strong like someone out of a romance novel?"

"Not really handsome," Ann stated with a shrug. "He was just what you'd call an ordinary sort of guy. There was nothing outstanding about him, except that he was tall with large hands and was solidly built. He also had beautiful blue eyes, blue like the waters in the South Pacific, at least from what her journals mentioned. Anyway, when the Chinese court handed down their ultimatum as to the only way she could gain her freedom was through pregnancy, they eventually allowed Luke to marry her. The court tribunal told her if she was lucky she'd have a baby boy and be released. There was never any mention as to what might become of her if she had a girl."

"So Eliza married Luke?" Dickey asked.

"Yes, she did," his mother said. "They were married in 1907 and fortunately, she had a baby boy that year while still in prison. For whatever reason, the authorities stuck by their word, which she and Luke never thought would ever come to pass, and she was released. It was a tough few months for them however, while waiting for her release, with Luke trying to work and care for her and the baby. Once she was free, her health over the next few months, instead of improving, failed miserably because of the harsh treatment she had suffered over the years. She eventually contracted tuberculosis, and was confined to a deplorable hospital for close to two years on an island off the coast of China. Today, if a person is diagnosed with tuberculosis it's generally controlled with medication. In those days they shuffled people off to what they called a sanitarium where they would be locked up and have no exposure or contact with the outside world. All the while Luke took care of the baby as best he could. By the time the doctors claimed Eliza was cured their baby was a toddler. Six months later, after she had gained back some of her strength and health, Luke signed on as an able bodied seaman on another trade ship sailing for the United States. After much begging he was allowed to take Eliza and the baby with him. It wasn't the best of living conditions on board ship, and it was only a step up from her prison cell. They lived in the hold of the ship for over ninety days on the journey."

"Where did they go in the United States?" Kelly asked, her eyes wide with excitement.

"San Francisco," Ann replied. "It was quite a journey for them, especially with a baby while enduring fierce pacific storms and rough seas. Three months later they arrived in the states. Eliza, under Luke's care and for whatever reason, was in much better health when they docked and had gained back most of her weight. They set up housekeeping in a small, two-room cold water flat just south of the piers. Luke actively sought work and gained temporary, but fairly steady employment, working on the docks. It was hard work and long hours, but the pay was good, and they needed the money."

"So their life turned out pretty good," Dickey asked feeling relieved.

"In manner of speaking," Ann replied solemnly, her eyes fixed on the floor.

"In an manner of speaking?" Dickey asked appearing confused. "What's that supposed to mean?"

"Well," Ann said, "Eliza always missed her home on Cape Cod. Even though she had left home at a young age and traveled the world seeing so many exotic places, Cape Cod still stuck in her mind and held a special place in her heart. She vowed someday she'd return to Cape Cod and settle down."

"And did she? I mean did she ever return?" Dickey asked. The image of what he and Charlie had seen that night at the lighthouse still haunted him. Had she actually returned, or was his father right when he said, the apparition he and Charlie had seen was nothing more than someone playing a bad joke on them?

"Her parents still kept in touch by writing letters to her over the years," Ann said, "and still kept a light burning in the window of Rocky Neck Lighthouse for her safe return, but she didn't come home right away. Actually it was thirty years later before she came back, not until after her husband, Luke, passed away peacefully one night in his sleep. They had a long and wonderful marriage and their only child, their son, Lucas, was now a full-grown man and a respected ship builder on the west coast. Over the years – after her husband's death – Eliza became pretty much of a recluse and never left the house unless absolutely necessary. Eventually at his mother's insistence, and due to her failing health from the effects her body had suffered over the years, Lucas, sold his ship building business in the late 1930's and moved her back to Cape Cod. He even tried to buy her a house here in Crystal Falls where she had grown up, but there was nothing available, so they settled in Mayport."

Dickey and Kelly sat mesmerized staring at their mother. There was something that nagged at Dickey, something that didn't make sense, and yet something that did.

Ann continued. "One night in 1944, Eliza had a premonition and begged Lucas to take her to the lighthouse."

"Premonition?" Dickey asked, cocking his head. "Meaning what?"

Ann glanced at her husband, Adam, and he nodded urging her to continue. "She had an odd feeling, *a premonition*, she wasn't going to last too much longer, and wanted to visit the lighthouse where she grew up, one last time before she…"

"Died?" Kelly asked finishing her mother's statement. A guarded smile crossed Ann's lips as she nodded. "What happened then, Mom?"

"Lucas tried in vain to talk her out of going out that night," Ann said, "because she wasn't feeling good, but most of all because the weather was so terrible. It was a totally moonless night and a heavy fog had settled in over Muffin Bay, and the rain was driving across the bay in horizontal sheets. Eliza was determined however, and off they went to Rocky Neck Lighthouse. Once there, she saw that nothing much had changed since she lived there as a child, except for the light that still glowed in the second floor window. It was still there and burning just as brightly as her parents had told her in their letters. I think in a way she felt comfort in that."

"And her parents had...?"

"Yes," Ann said anticipating Dickey's question. "Her parent's had passed away years before and are buried up at Tall Oaks Cemetery, the one on the large hill just past your school." She paused locking her fingers together in her lap. "Actually, it's where all the Denton's are buried."

"What...happened to Eliza, Mom?" Kelly asked in a hushed whisper.

"As she had envisioned in her premonition," Ann said, "Eliza passed away that wild and stormy night while at the lighthouse with her only son, Lucas, at her side. It wasn't anything dramatic—she just sat down on the deacon's bench on the second floor to catch her breath from the climb up—and closed her eyes."

Kelly's mouth hung open, her eyes fixed on her mother. "So her spirit really *does* inhabit Rocky Neck Lighthouse?" She swallowed hard anticipating her mother's answer.

Ann nodded. "Yes, her spirit really *does* inhabit the lighthouse, but like your father said, not in the form that Dickey thought he saw. What

Dickey and Charlie most likely saw was some friend of theirs making believe he was a ghost staggering around in a sheet with his arms outstretched like you'd see in a comedy horror movie." Dickey tried to speak but nothing came out. His mother noticed his apprehension and directed her attention to him. "If you had *truly* seen Eliza, Dickey," she stated, "her spirit would have been more like a deep cool fog swaying gently with a warm white glow surrounding her spirit. People who have witnessed her spirit claim they can actually feel the change in temperature in the room when her spirit appears. She's not there to frighten people; she's simply there to complete her journey. And to be close to her parents whom she left so abruptly that cold winter night in December so many years ago."

"And Dickey," Adam broke in, "if you had actually seen her like your mother said, you would remember it because her only distinguishing feature would've plainly stood out. A beauty mark, right here," he said touching his index finger to his left cheek.

Dickey felt like he was going to faint dead away. Adam nervously cleared his throat and wet down his cowlick before continuing. "The reason we have confided all this information to both of you," he said in a hushed tone, "and the reason I told you this was important for you to know, is that Eliza's son, Lucas is...my grandfather."

Kelly and Dickey sat stunned; the wicker chair squeaking noisily as Dickey uneasily adjusted his position.

Kelly thought long and hard for a moment and then finally spoke. Her expression was if someone had just lifted a curtain on the secret of the lighthouse. Her words were brief and to the point. "That would make

Eliza's son, Lucas, Grandpa's father, right, Dad?" Adam nodded and looked expectantly at Dickey.

"If that's true," Dickey remarked, his brow furrowing in thought. "That would make Lucas...her son...our great grandfather." He paused and thought for another long moment, and then a spark of understanding lit up his marble black eyes. It was apparent that the family secret was all becoming crystal clear. "Meaning...that's why Grandpa has Eliza's journals, because the young girl from the lighthouse, Eliza Tuffett, became Eliza Denton when she married Luke." His eyes narrowed as he stared intently at his mother. "Oh my goodness!" Dickey stammered, nervously running his tongue over his lips. "What you're trying to tell us is that Eliza Tuffett is somehow related to us."

"Not just *somehow* related, Dickey," Ann Denton remarked with a guarded smile. "Eliza Tuffett is your great great grandmother!"

Epilogue

Later, Dickey retired to his room. He was still trying to comprehend the gravity of what he had learned, while trying to accept the fact of exactly why his parents were so troubled about the existence of Eliza's spirit. *Maybe it bothers Mom and Dad*, he thought, but to me, having a real live ghost for a relative is just the neatest thing. It was something he could laud over any kid in class—even Bobby Page. He tried to put his parents' concern out of his head, but couldn't. Long before he learned that Eliza Tuffett was his great great grandmother, he had admired the adventurous life she had lived. He hoped sometime he would have the chance to see her spirit.

He knelt down and removed his sacred box that was taped securely under his dresser and carried it to his bed. Opening it, he stared at the gold button with the inscribed initials PH, recalling his adventure last year on Angel Island. After a moment he closed the box and set it on his lap, promising himself that if Grandpa came for Labor Day he would tell him the story of how they came to be rescued. Maybe Grandpa would even allow him to read more of Eliza's journals. There was so much more he wanted to know about her.

He knew there was a lot that his great great grandmother, Eliza, and the pirate, Peg Leg Pete, had in common. They had taught him to believe in himself and trust his judgment—and never, ever to be afraid of taking a journey beyond his wildest imagination.

But there was more—more he still hadn't disclosed to anyone— and yet, more importantly—when could he? And when, if ever, was he going to have the rare opportunity, and courage, to turn the knob on the front door of the Josiah Wheeler house?

He tucked the box back under his dresser, secured it tightly and leaned against the wall wondering about something that still nagged at him.

Who's to say that one spirit may even know another? *If we know each other in this world,* he mused, *then why not in another?* Maybe Charlie was right after all. Maybe this is what he meant by metaphysical.

A guarded smile crossed his lips, as he thought; *maybe it's time I find out.*

ABOUT THE AUTHOR

Rick Farren was born in 1939 in Boston, Massachusetts. As a young boy he and his family moved to Westchester County in New York, where he spent most of his childhood living on a farm.

Rick's parents helped shape his love of writing and adventure. His father was a sportswriter and a newspaper reporter. His father encouraged him to learn one new word each day. At the end of the week he had to write a story using each of the new words he had learned. His mother was a stunt pilot as well as a housewife. She always taught her children never to be afraid to try something new and exciting.

Rick's lifelong love of reading was influenced by poetry from, "A Child's Garden of Verses," western novels by Zane Gray, Grimm's Fairy Tales, poems by Henry Wadsworth Longfellow, and stories of pirates on the high seas.

When he was a teenager, his family moved back to Massachusetts and Rick attended Newton High School. After high school, Rick served in the US Air force in San Antonio Texas where he met his wife, Ann. Together they had 4 children and lived in Brockton, Massachusetts. Rick spent his career in the Banking and Financial Services industry and earned a Banking certificate from Brown University.

Presently he is retired and lives in West Falmouth, Massachusetts with his wife Ann. He is an active member of the Cape Cod Writer's Center and the Falmouth Theater Guild. He enjoys writing stories for his grandchildren, golfing, mystery writing, community theater and reading.

Journey Publications

ALSO AVAILABLE FROM
JOURNEY PUBLICATIONS

"Psychic Princess: Admirable Avocation" by *Jolinda Pizzirani* is the first in a series about a young woman with psychic abilities who unwillingly gets involved in solving various crimes. In this first volume, she follows her instincts to solve the kidnapping of a young girl from a wealthy family. She also gets married to the young policeman involved in the case, setting the scene for future stories where she is pulled into crime-solving, like it or not.

U. S. $15.95   ISBN: 0-9728716-2-4

"Practical Theories & Formulas for Engineering, Physics and Math" by Jorgen Andersson has been called "four years of engineering college in one book." With this book, you have knowledge and education at your fingertips to inspire you. During your educational studies, you may find the short examples with graphs helpful. If you have already finished your education, this book is a "one of a kind resource" to fall back on. Enhance your knowledge by rediscovering the creativity in mathematics and its applications.

U.S. $19.50 / CAN. $25.50   ISBN: 0-9748087-2-5

Order Any of These Great Books from:
www.journeypublications.com, www.barnesandnoble.com, www.amazon.com or find them in your local bookstore!
Email JourneyPubs@aol.com for more information.

Journey Publications, P. O. Box 1071, Summerland, CA 93067 PH: (805) 565-0525